EMPTY WORLD

A POST-APOCALYPTIC THRILLER

ZACH BOHANNON

MOLTEN
UNIVERSE

Edited by Jennifer Collins

Proofread by Robert Pettigrew

Cover by Roy Migabon

zachbohannon.com
moltenuniversemedia.com

AUTHOR'S NOTE

Just a quick note before you get started...

Empty World takes place 30 years after the events of my six-book series, Empty Bodies. While longtime fans of that series will find little Easter eggs throughout this novel, you do not have to have read those books to enjoy this. Empty World stands on its own.

If you would like to read the original series, either before you start this novel or after, you can pick up the first book at http://books2read.com/emptybodies

So with that, to new readers, and to all the Empties out there... welcome to Empty World.

-Zach

For all the Empties out there. This one's for you.

1

Every morning when Shell Langford woke, she gave the honor to the same knife of making a new mark on the wall.

Flipping the silver blade over in her hand and taking hold of the inscribed, bone handle, Shell carved another notch into the stark-white drywall.

1,925 days alone.

She scanned the wall, each cut of the blade representing another day she'd survived. And with some luck, she'd be there to carve a new mark the next day. For now, it was time to go outside and do her day's chores.

She walked outside and down her porch steps to make the trek across the yard to the barn. Not a single cloud blocked the sun, and it illuminated the inside of the barn as Shell pulled the doors all the way open. It shone throughout the area, lighting up the faces of the goats. Aside from the chickens in their pen on the other end of the yard, the goats were the only animals she had left.

At the pen, she put her dark brown hair into a ponytail, then she slid the bolt aside to open the gate.

"Good morning, friends."

The two male goats made their way from their bed of straw and wandered out the large barn doors to go stretch their legs in the fenced-in yard.

When they were out, Shell took hold of the nanny goat, whom she had named Lisa. She led her to the center of the barn and up onto the milking stand, then placed a bucket under the goat. Then she squatted and pulled at the goat's teats and milk flowed down into the bucket.

As she extracted the morning's supply from Lisa, Shell looked back into the pasture. The other goats grazed in the newly greened grass, picking mostly at weeds. Winter had been one of the most treacherous in Shell's twenty-three years, or at least in the eighteen or nineteen that she could remember. She hadn't been sure that all the animals would make it through the cold, but she'd been fortunate—the only loss had been two of her chickens. With Spring now here, she hoped to have a few weeks of decent temperatures before the Mississippi heat began cursing her day in and day out for several months.

When she finished milking Lisa, she helped the goat off the stand, petting her on the back.

"You're a good girl, Lisa."

The goat bleated back at her, and Shell smiled. She led the animal out into the field with the others. Shell picked up the bucket of milk, along with her bow and quiver of arrows, then left the barn and made her way back to her house to drop the milk off.

As she headed across the meadow, she glanced over to the vegetable garden. Out of the corner of her eye, she saw something. Shell paused, jerking her head in that direction. She squinted her eyes and focused, but it turned out to only be a rabbit, hopping under the fence at the edge of the yard. Shell smiled and shook her head. Even though it had been a long time since she'd seen a Dead or a person, that didn't keep her mind from playing tricks on her and leaving her paranoid. But as was usual, it was no threat.

Shell walked up the porch steps, dropping the bucket of milk off on the patio and picking up an empty basket. Then she made her way over to the chicken coop.

She arrived and dropped her bow and arrows on the ground, then opened the doors to the shack, the chickens clucking as she entered. Shell moved down the row, collecting eggs into the basket. The seven chickens had produced a total of five eggs—enough for her to eat over the next couple of days.

When Shell had finished collecting the eggs, she opened the doors to let the chickens out into the vast, caged area so they could move around and get some sun.

Picking up the basket and her bow and quiver, Shell exited out the front of the coop and headed back toward the house. She needed to get her milk and eggs inside the before she went to tend to the vegetable garden.

Shell was halfway back to the house and looking down at the ground when she heard a rustling come from the yard. She glanced over and watched as a shirtless young boy stood at her garden some twenty yards away. Shell narrowed her eyes, her jaw slack. The boy staring at her couldn't have been more than eight years old. He was covered in dirt, his face hardly recognizable under the muck and the ragged mop of hair on top of his head. In one of his hands, he held a bag, and in the other was a potato. Shell's potato.

The boy ran.

Shell set down her basket of eggs and gave chase. Even with his short legs, the boy was fast. Shell thought to drop her bow, but she was worried the boy might not be alone. What if there were others waiting on the road where he was headed? She didn't want to come across a gang and be weaponless, even though the boy was the first person she had seen in at least two years.

She ran across the yard to the road, a hundred and fifty feet from the front of the house. The boy was much faster than her, making his head start more of a disadvantage for her.

The boy reached the road as Shell called out to him.

"Stop!"

But the boy ignored her.

He reached a bicycle, adjusting the bag so he could hop on. This delay allowed Shell to catch up to him some. But when she was still several dozen feet away, he took off, pedaling slowly at first, but then coasting down the steep hill that started only fifteen yards from her driveway.

Shell reached the top of the hill behind him, out of breath, and she watched the boy pick up speed as he moved down it. He glanced over his shoulder every so often to make sure she wasn't following him. She leaned on her knees, fighting to catch her breath as she watched the boy speed away from her with the stolen crops.

When the boy had ridden out of her sight and her heart rate had lowered, Shell stood up straight and walked back to the yard, arriving back at the garden. Taking inventory, she realized that the boy had stolen most of what she would've been able to harvest that day. From what she could tell, he had even ripped out of the ground some of the premature vegetable plants. Exhaling a heavy sigh, Shell clenched her eyes shut. There was nothing she could do about the stolen vegetables. She could only hope to salvage what was left.

But she now had to worry about someone knowing where she was. She had dealt with wildlife getting into her garden. Rabbits and the occasional wild dog had been mostly easy to deal with through setting humane traps and making sure she maintained the chicken-wire fence around the garden. She'd even managed to keep the Deads away. But a living, breathing human was a different story.

The thought that the boy might not be alone returned to her. If he were part of a gang or a family, they would surely return.

And when that happened, Shell would be ready.

2

SHELL RETURNED the chickens to the coop and then made her way over to the barn to gather the goats. Typically, she would allow the goats to graze for most of the day, but she was paranoid since that boy had shown up earlier.

After locking the goats away, Shell jogged back to the house. She went straight to her garage and opened the fishing tackle box sitting on a shelf. She pulled out a spool of fishing line before going back into the house.

Hurrying up the stairs, she pulled the rope on the ceiling to open the attic and climbed up. She looked around at the dusty cardboard boxes until she found the one she was looking for. It had been marked 'Xmas' with a permanent black marker, though the label had faded over time. Opening it, she found an array of Christmas ornaments. The box probably hadn't been out of the attic since she was six or seven years old.

Shell shifted through the box until she heard what she was looking for. At the bottom of the box were sleigh bells, as well as some jingle bells on a ribbon.

She took her finds to the kitchen and set the ornaments

on the table. Then, Shell sat down and removed the bells one by one, setting them in a row on the ground. By the time she'd finished, she had thirty-eight silver bells. She gathered them into a plastic bag, threw her bow and quiver over her shoulder, and went back over to her vegetable garden.

Stretching out the fishing line, she tied one end to a sturdy bush, making sure it was less than a foot off the ground. She then walked backward, stretching the wire across the front of her vegetable garden. She stopped only when she reached a tree, setting the wire on the ground in front of it. Then she spent the next several minutes tying most of the bells onto the wire. When she was done, she tied the other end of the wire around the tree. She retrieved her bag, then headed for the chicken coop.

The entire walk over she kept a lookout, anticipating that the boy would return. Though she knew he was unlikely to come back the same day, he was a child. And children were unpredictable.

At the chicken coop, she tied the bells around the handle on the door. Then she went over to the barn and did the same. If he came back, Shell was going to be alerted.

When she finished rigging the two doors, she went back to the garden and looked at the wire. It was unlikely an invader would miss it during the day, but she hoped that her presence that morning would have inspired the boy to return at night when she was sleeping, if at all. There was no way he would see any of the noisemakers with only the moon's light to guide him. Hopefully, this would be enough to scare the boy off from coming back again.

With things as secure as she could make them, Shell retrieved her bow and quiver and walked across the yard to her practice area. She'd painted a target on the largest tree on the property, the same tree she'd climbed so often as a young girl. Occasionally, she'd still climb into the tree now, but it was mostly there to hone her bow skills, and to provide her a shady place to read a book on cooler days.

Target practice gave her the opportunity to clear her mind. She focused on her breathing, letting arrow after arrow fly from her bow to the tree trunk. Today it was much harder to clear her mind, though. She kept thinking of the boy, wondering if and when he'd come back. After only about ten minutes shooting and unable to ease her racing mind, she decided to go back into the house and rest for a while.

As she reached the two-story farmhouse, Shell's attention turned to the small cemetery on the other side of it. She hesitated before dropping her bow and quiver on the porch steps. She picked three freshly bloomed flowers she'd planted in front of the house, then walked over to the graves.

Shell had done her best to keep up the maintenance around the graves. With Spring just arriving again, she knew she would have much work to do in order to keep the cemetery neat. Shell had fashioned the grave markers out of wood, knowing it was all she'd had, and had carved the names into them with a knife. She walked amongst the graves now, running her hand along the top of several of the wooden markers as she read the names. Remembered the faces.

There were over a dozen graves in all, belonging to the people who had once lived in all the surrounding houses, and in hers.

After looking at several of the grave markings, she stopped at a particular plot.

LEWIS ROBINSON
DIED MAY 2, 2038

FRIEND AND MENTOR

Shell smiled, setting one of the flowers down in front of the grave.

"Thank you for all you taught me. I have only survived as long as I have because of you."

She kissed two of her fingers and then touched the wooden marker, just above the name. Then she stood.

Stepping around more graves, Shell arrived at the other two she visited when she made it to this side of the house.

MICHELLE LANGFORD
BORN DECEMBER 20, 1995
DIED MAY 15, 2021
BELOVED MOTHER AND WIFE

ROBERT "BOBBY" LANGFORD
BORN AUGUST 8, 1993
DIED AUGUST 3, 2027
BELOVED FATHER AND HUSBAND

She kneeled down between the graves of her parents. She did not—could not—speak. She instead remained silent, running her hand over the grass. Tears formed in her eyes and she sniffled, raising her arm to her face to wipe away the tears. With glassy eyes, she looked up and stared at the two names. This was the first time in several visits she had cried. Perhaps it was the sight of the boy earlier in the day that was getting to her. It had been so long since she'd seen another living human that she had almost forgotten what others looked like, especially children.

After several minutes of reflection and prayer, Shell lay the other two flowers on her mother's and father's graves respectively, then stood. A breeze blew through the air, cooling her skin as she turned her back to the graves. She walked back around to the front and picked up her bow and arrows as she headed up the porch stairs and into the house.

Shell spent the rest of the morning and afternoon relaxing inside, reading a book and occasionally glancing out the window to see if anyone was there. Her paranoia was real, and nothing she did could keep her mind off of the boy.

It wasn't until later in the afternoon that she went back outside to feed the chickens and goats and to milk Lisa a second time. On her way back inside, she checked the wires once more to make sure they were tight, then headed back to the house. The sun was in the horizon now, the sky painted in shades of purple and orange. She appreciated the beauty in it, and as she walked back to the house and looked over at the grave markers at the side of the house, she wondered if her parents and Lewis were watching over her. She smiled, then went back into the house.

Though it was one of Spring's first days, the inside of the farmhouse was chilly that night. This was fine by Shell, as she could simply start a fire to provide both heat and light. She could save the candles she had for warmer evenings when a fire would be unnecessary. With months of humid nights ahead, she'd gladly enjoy the Spring temperatures while she could.

She kept a small stack of firewood next to the fireplace, and she threw a couple of logs inside. While getting the wood required the labor of chopping, starting the fire once the logs were inside was easy. Between all the houses in the small Mississippi Delta town, Shell had gathered enough matches and lighters to last her probably another ten years. Her father had often joked how this stockpile was the only thing that had ever made him thankful so many people had smoked cigarettes.

Shell lit the fire, then went to the kitchen to grab a glass of milk, two carrots, and a potato which would be her dinner. Then she plopped down onto the couch to relax and eat. Physically, the day had been less taxing on her body than many others. Taking care of the animals and her garden were everyday tasks she was used to, but this had mentally been one of the hardest days she'd had in a while. Over and over in her mind, Shell saw that boy's grime-covered face. She replayed the scene of him cruising down the hill on the bike, looking back at her as she worked to catch her breath.

Glancing out the nearby window, she noted that the clear sky allowed the moon to truly illuminate the yard. Though it was dark, from where she sat, she could see the silhouettes of the vegetable garden and the barn.

As her mind continued to wander over the next hour, she knew there was only one way to turn it off. She stood up and put out the fire before heading upstairs to her bedroom.

There were four bedrooms upstairs, and Shell's looked out over the front yard, giving her a clear view of the vegetable garden and the barn. She mounted her bow to the hooks above her chest of drawers, then set the quiver of arrows on top of that next to her knife. Then she cracked the window on the far wall enough to where she would hear the boy if he returned. Breathing in the fresh air, she looked out over the garden, the chicken shack, and the barn. If the boy came back, she would know it.

Shell crawled on top of the mattress, remaining in her clothes so that she'd be prepared to run outside if she had to.

Her gaze fell upon the wall across the room as she lay

down. Ever since the day Lewis had died, Shell had made a mark on the wall each morning to keep track of how long she had been alone. The marks covered most of the wall now. They made her think of the boy again, wondering if he were alone as well.

Her mind continued to race as she lay on her side, focusing her attention out the window.

But her exhaustion soon caught up with her, and then Shell slept.

3

SHELL AWOKE when she heard the bells ringing in the meadow. She rolled from her bed and looked outside. Near the vegetable garden, she saw the silhouette of a figure standing under the moon's light.

She grabbed her bow and ran down the stairs and out the front door.

As she hurried down the porch stairs and into the front yard, she looked toward the garden to see that it wasn't just one figure standing there, but two. Neither was the size of the boy—they were closer to her height. She drew an arrow from the quiver on her back and nocked it into the bow's rest. Slowly, she moved toward the two shadows.

"Don't move. I swear, I'll shoot. Put your hands in the air."

Neither figure did as she asked, instead remaining still. Shell continued toward them.

"Don't test me!"

"You're not going to shoot."

Shell stopped. The string of the bow pulled taut, she tilted her head as she recognized the male voice.

The shadow moved toward her, but she remained where she was with the arrow pointed at him. Shell's attention turned only when the light above the barn doors came on bright enough to illuminate much of her yard. She had never seen the light work. She'd never seen any lightbulb work. And when she turned back to the shadow, she saw that the light shone upon a familiar face.

"Dad?"

Shell's father smiled as he looked back at his daughter. "Hi, Bear."

Hearing the nickname her father had called her until the day he'd passed, Shell felt tears fill her eyes. She lowered the bow, dumbfounded that her father stood before her.

She froze in disbelief, before muttering, "Daddy?" Then she ran into his open arms, clenching her eyes shut as he ran his hands up and down her back, holding her tight.

"Hello, Shell."

Shell opened her eyes to see her mother standing several feet behind her father. She pulled away from him and her father stepped aside.

She ran to her mother next, hugging her as she had her father.

After several moments embracing them, Shell pulled away. "I'm dreaming."

Her mother nodded.

A sudden disappointment passed over Shell. "But it feels so real." She looked back to her father. "The hugs. Your faces. It's all so real."

"Do you remember the last thing I said to you, Bear?" her father asked.

Shell nodded. "I think of it every single day, Dad. You said, 'Glance into the sky, put your hand over your heart, and your mother and I will always be here.'"

Her father smiled. "And here we are."

"But I want this to be real."

"Our spirits live inside of you," her mother said. "I can't begin to tell you how proud I am of the woman you have become."

Shell lowered her head. "I want us to be together."

A hand grabbed onto her shoulder then and she looked up to see her father. "And we will be. But not anytime soon. You have to live on. To survive. There will be an eternity to spend with us, Bear."

With tears flowing now, Shell lowered her head and nodded. The grip left her shoulder, and she looked up to see her father and mother walking away from her.

"Don't leave."

"We have to, sweetie," her mother said. "It's time for you to wake up."

"I don't want to wake up. Ever."

Her father looked back. "Just remember." He looked to the sky, then placed his hand over his heart. Smiling at her one last time, he turned around.

She watched her parents walk into the barn's light and disappear, as the white light then expanded to fill the space all around her.

SHELL SHOT up off the pillow, gasping for air. Beads of sweat slid down her cheeks and her entire body felt hot. She'd perspired through her clothing, her faded gray t-shirt sticking to her. Throwing her legs over the side of the bed, she wiped her brow. Then, resting her elbows on her knees, she drew in deep breaths.

The dream had felt so real. Her hands trembled as she

tried to shake it off. She brought her face out of her palms and looked into the mirror across the room. Her face was flush of any color, and the bags under her eyes made her appear as if she hadn't slept in days. She had tossed and turned all night before dreaming of her parents. It was early morning now, the sun peeking over the horizon.

She still sat reflecting on the dream when the bells went off outside.

Shell hurried to the window.

It was the boy.

He stood near the garden, frozen. He looked toward the house and Shell ducked out of the window, throwing her back against the adjacent wall.

When she looked outside again, the boy was running away.

This time, he wouldn't escape.

Shell grabbed her bow, arrows, and knife, then headed down the stairs.

By the time Shell made it out the front door, the boy had run out of sight. Assuming he would flee the same way he had the last time, Shell ran for the road again.

By the time she made it there, the boy had already mounted his bike. He looked back as Shell ran onto the road, and he sped up at the sight of her.

"Stop!"

Determined not to allow the boy to evade her again, Shell took chase. He started down the hill again, but she came after him this time, running down the hill as he pulled away.

The boy kept glancing back to make sure he was distancing himself from Shell. He was, but she breathed heavily and tried to gain ground.

The boy was looking back when he rounded a corner.

Shell saw the figure ahead of him before he did and she called out to warn him. The boy turned around just in time to swerve away from the lumbering Dead coming down the street. He fell off the bike, crying out and sliding on the pavement for a moment before coming to a stop. The boy took hold of his skinned knee, and Shell saw that he had the creature's attention now—it had turned to go for the boy.

Shell came within fifteen yards of the Dead before she stopped, drew an arrow from her quiver, and nocked it. Pulling back on the bowstring, she aimed, steadying her breathing so that her hands didn't shake. She drew in a deep breath then, puffing her chest before she exhaled. As she pushed the breath out of her lungs, Shell let go.

The arrow flew through the air, whistling along with the boy's scream. It caught the Dead in the skull, running through the top of its earlobe, and the creature toppled to the pavement.

With wide eyes, the boy looked at the creature, then back up at Shell. He fought to stand up, but one of his legs had gotten tangled in the frame of his bike. Shell hurried over to him as he worked to free himself.

When Shell reached him, the boy froze, trembling and staring into her face.

"Stay still."

Shell lifted the bike for him then, maneuvering it to where he could pull his leg out.

"Can you move it?"

The boy nodded, then grimaced as he moved his leg, bending it at the knee to remove it from the spaces between the bike's frame. When he was loose, he returned his hands to his skinned knee.

"Let me see," Shell said, urging the boy to move his hands.

He did, revealing severe scrapes on both legs. His knees had matching wounds, and his left shin had a three-inch cut that bled.

"We've got to clean this up. What's your name?"

The boy didn't respond. He didn't even look at her, keeping his eyes focused on his legs.

"All right, well, are you going to stay here while I run back to the house and grab some supplies to patch you up with?"

Again, the boy said nothing.

Shell sighed. "Well, all I want to do is help you, if that isn't apparent from me taking that Dead down before it killed you. So, hopefully you'll stay here." She stood up.

Reaching to her waist, she took hold of her knife. She pulled it out and looked at it. Flipping it in her hand, she gripped it by the blade and then extended it toward the boy.

Confusion crossed his face.

"In case another one of those things shows up. I want you to be able to defend yourself." She also wanted to show the boy that she was no threat to him.

The boy waited a moment, then accepted the weapon with a trembling hand.

Shell went to the Dead, removing the arrow from its skull. Returning it to her quiver, she turned back to the boy.

"I'll be back."

4

SHELL BUSTED through her front door and hurried up the stairs. She entered the room at the end of the hall and opened the closet door. Not long after Lewis died, she'd moved the first-aid supplies upstairs into the bedroom closet, converting it into a large medical cabinet. She regularly slept on the top floor, and she'd wanted the first aid to be nearby. Aside from her animals, they were her most prized possessions.

She reached for the designated shelf and found gauze, bandages of an appropriate size to cover the boy's wounds, and peroxide. Downstairs, she grabbed some rags out of her kitchen. Then, with the items cupped in her arms, Shell headed back outside.

When she reached the road, the boy hadn't moved. He'd remained seated next to his bike, leaning back on his hands. He bit his lip, keeping a stern stare at Shell.

Ignoring the boy's scowl, Shell kneeled down next to him. She set her first aid items down, then picked up one of the rags from the stack of supplies. She wiped the blood away that had run down his legs, applying enough pressure to clean away any residue. When she arrived at the wounds, she let up some of the pressure. Still, the boy grimaced as the dry rag made contact with the open cuts.

"Sorry."

The boy was, again, unresponsive, but Shell continued to wipe away the blood. When she'd cleared away as much as she could, she reached over and grabbed the bottle of peroxide. The boy stared at the brown bottle, and she could see it wasn't anything he recognized. Shell shook it, finding that it was half-full. Thinking back to the closet, she remembered seeing two unopened bottles.

As she unscrewed the top, Shell shook her head. "This isn't going to feel good, but we have to make sure these cuts don't get infected." She grabbed one of the clean rags and extended it toward the boy. "Bite down on this."

The boy's stare was unfazed. Shell simply shrugged.

"Suit yourself."

When the liquid hit the open wound, the boy jumped and cried out. He swiped the rag from Shell's hand and bit down on it, gritting his teeth so hard that a vein in his forehead bulged.

"Take deep breaths," Shell said. "This'll only take a minute."

When she finished cleaning out the cuts with the peroxide, Shell began the task of covering each cut. She wrapped the more serious wounds with gauze, using tape to keep them in place. Then she covered the more minor cuts with small bandages.

When Shell finished, she leaned back and observed her work. Her eyes met the boy's, and she smiled at him.

"You did a great job. You're tough."

The boy looked away from her, but Shell noticed that with the dirt on his face, she could see him blushing. Shell maneuvered her head so that he was forced to look at her. She smiled again.

"I see you blushing. Don't try and hide it."

The boy's face got redder.

"Now, will you tell me your name?"

As if the question were a knife, the boy's smile disappeared. He dropped his eyes to the ground again, his hair draping over his face, but shook his head this time.

"You don't have a name?"

Again, he shook his head.

"Where are your parents?"

His head shook again.

"Can you talk?"

No response. The boy refused to look at her now.

"I'm sorry. I'll stop asking questions."

The boy lifted his eyes to Shell's, apparently satisfied by the gesture.

"What do you say we get you back to my house? I would assume you have to be hungry since you've been stealing from my garden."

The boy nodded, and Shell smiled. She stood up, then offered the boy a hand in getting to his feet.

"Are we invited to this party?"

Shell had been looking down when the gruff voice spoke behind her. She whipped her head around to see a group of seven men on the road. They all rode on horses.

One horse stood in front of the others, and the man riding on top of it hopped off the animal. He had olive skin and wore a scraggly beard on his face that matched the consistency of his stringy hair. His hair came to his shoulder and blended with the unkempt beard.

Shell moved to stand in front of the boy, shielding him from the men. The apparent leader of the group smiled.

"What's the matter?" he asked.

"Just tell me what you want," Shell said.

He laughed. "Want? We just want to be friends."

"I don't need any friends."

He pointed to the boy. "Seems like you were being awfully friendly to the boy there. How about we start with names? I'm Ray."

Shell backed up and took the boy by the hand.

"We don't want to hurt you, do we, fellas?"

The men behind Ray shook their heads, wide grins spread across their faces.

"Then tell me what you want."

Ray narrowed his eyes and stuck his arms out, letting them fall to his sides as he shrugged. "I thought I told you. I want us to be friends. And I thought that maybe if we were friends, you'd allow us to come have a look at your place."

"Go to hell."

The gang all laughed along with Ray.

Fed up with the men, Shell reached down and snatched the knife back from the boy. Ray moved back a few steps, chuckling still. He put his palms out toward her.

"Whoa, easy."

Shell held the boy behind her as she aimed the knife at the men. Then she watched as each of the men behind Ray pulled out their own weapons. One man pulled out a sword. Another an ax. The other two held baseball bats. Ray remained standing in front of the men, a grin stretched across his face.

"I don't see that you have much choice in the matter. Now, put down the knife and the bow. That is, if you don't want us to hurt the boy."

Shell glanced down at the boy. His face remained stoic, focused on the gang, and he still held onto her hand.

With no other choice, Shell exhaled and tossed the knife near Ray's feet.

"Good," Ray said. "Now the bow."

Shell pulled the bow around and dropped it to the ground. Shrugging her shoulder, she allowed the quiver to drop off her shoulder and fall to the pavement next.

"Very good," Ray said. He then looked over his shoulder and gestured to his men. The other men dismounted their horses. One grabbed Shell by the arm, and another took hold of the boy, while the other four men took the reins of the horses.

"Let me go!" Shell said.

Ray leaned toward her face. "Not until you've given me my tour."

5

"Just look at this fucking place, boys."

The men continued to hold onto Shell as Ray stood near the house, looking out into the meadow. He glanced back at her.

"There's no way it's only a pretty girl like yourself out here with all this land."

Shell averted her eyes.

"Damn," Ray said, laughing. "I mean, you've grown food, and you've got goats and chickens. You've been busy." He looked up toward the house, then out into the field again, using his hands as a visor to shield his eyes from the risen sun. "I know there's some nice houses in this town, but the rest of the boys are gonna have to fight me over this place."

Shell's heart skipped a beat. "What do you mean?"

"Well, you're just a little girl. You think we're going to let you live out here in this town by yourself?"

"This is my home," Shell said. "And I'm not a little girl. I'm twenty-three."

"Young and feisty. Just how I like 'em."

"Screw you." Shell spit, and it hit Ray in the cheek.

As he wiped it away, one of the nearby men reached over and backhanded her across the face. He had to have at least a hundred pounds on Shell, and his large hand felt like a rock slamming into her cheek.

Ray marched toward his man and pushed him away from Shell. "What the fuck are you doing?"

"She can't talk to us like that."

"Hit her again, and I'll fucking kill you. You got that?" Ray was inches from the man's face.

"Yeah, dude. Chill."

Ray turned to Shell. She held her cheek, trying to rub away the pain.

"And if you spit on me again, I'll do things to you that you couldn't imagine in your worst nightmare. Do you understand me?"

Shell acknowledged him only with a slight nod. The crooked smile returned to his face.

"Look around," Ray said to his men. "See what all you can find." He then looked to a man in his twenties with blonde hair. "Cody, I want you to head back and tell the others what we found. In the meanwhile, Miss Bad Ass here is gonna give me a tour through the house, then around town." He gestured to the man holding the boy. "Stay out here with him."

The other men scattered, including Cody, who jumped on his horse and raced across the yard to the highway. Ray grabbed Shell's arm and led her up the porch and into the house. They entered the front room.

"Damn, girl. Look at this place. You've been staying here all by yourself? Really?"

Shell didn't respond, and the smile left Ray's face again.

"I didn't want to have to show you this, girl, but you've left me no choice."

He reached to his back, under his jacket, and pulled out a handgun. Shell hadn't seen someone fire a gun since she'd been a little girl. The town had run out of ammo long ago, back when seeing Deads had been a more regular thing. She stared at the gun in the man's hand. Again, his smile returned.

"I'm sure that, even at your age, you know what this is and what it can do."

"You're lying," Shell said, a tremble in her voice. "I'll bet that thing doesn't even fire."

Ray pointed the gun at her, stopping inches from her forehead. "You want to find out?" He moved his thumb, and the gun clicked. "That was the sound of a bullet going into the chamber. It's my last one, and I've been saving it for a special occasion. All I have to do now is pull this trigger, and we can see just how much of a liar I am."

Sweat collected on Shell's brow. Her body quaked, but she didn't allow herself to cry or for her hard gaze to leave the man. He tilted his head.

"You're a tough girl." He lowered the gun. "I have to say that I admire that. Now are you going to be polite and show me around, or not?"

Shell continued to stare at him. Knowing she had no other choice, she led him into the kitchen first.

"Don't try anything stupid. I promise I'll shoot you before you can even turn around."

Stopping in the kitchen, Shell turned around. Ray studied the room for a moment before rummaging through the cabinets and drawers. Most of them were filled with dishes Shell hardly used. He looked in the pantry where Shell kept some of the food she had harvested and then canned. He grabbed a jar of corn and turned around.

"You did all this yourself?"

Shell nodded.

Still holding the jar in his hand, Ray went to her.

"You better not be lying to me about being the only one here. Because if you are, I'm going to make you watch them die before I kill you."

"It's just me. I swear."

He raised an eyebrow before turning around and returning the jar to the pantry.

"You patched the boy up with bandages and peroxide. Where did you get those things from? I didn't see them in the cabinets."

Shell averted her eyes, staring down at the linoleum tile. Her food, medicine, and everything she had collected over the years would soon be gone. She dreaded starting over but knew there was no way this ended without the men overtaking her house and keeping all the things here for themselves.

"Tell me," Ray said, snapping Shell out of her thoughts.

"They're in a closet upstairs."

He stood up straight, sticking out his arms and grinning. "Perfect! I was just thinking we should head up there."

Ray followed Shell up the stairs. Her heart raced as she continued to ponder what her life would be like once these men took her house over. If they let her go, where would she go? She couldn't stay there. Without her home, she'd have no milk from her goats. No eggs from her chickens. No fresh vegetables to eat.

When they reached the closet door, Shell stopped.

"Is this the one?" Ray asked.

She turned around to him, tears forming in her eyes for the first time. "Please don't take my things. They're all I have to survive."

Ray put his hands on his hips. "I guess you'll just have to find another way to survive then, won't you?"

"I've worked so hard to gather things from all over the town. There's nothing left. I'll die."

"Everything you've worked for: it's ours now. I'm sorry, but that's just the way it's going to be."

He went to move past her, but Shell blocked the door.

Ray tilted his head and furrowed his brow. "Don't do this. You're not going to win."

"I can't let you take my food and my medicine. My home."

"You don't have a choice. Now, move."

He grabbed her shoulder to push her away, and Shell bit the top of his hand. Ray let out a gut-wrenching scream as Shell felt the warm blood gather around her lips. She released her teeth and then pushed him aside as she ran for the stairs.

Shell plowed through the front door only to find the other men gathered at the bottom of the porch stairs. When she turned around again, Ray was coming through the living room, and he threw the screen door open nearly hard enough to break it off its hinges. Teeth gritted, he let go of his wounded hand and grabbed Shell by the back of her shirt. Without a care, he pushed her down the stairs.

Shell tumbled, landing on her hands and knees at the bottom of the porch steps. She writhed, rolling onto her back. Boots creaked down the wooden porch steps and, when she looked up, Ray stood above her, blocking out the sun as he pointed the gun at her.

"You stupid bitch. I told you not to try anything. But you couldn't listen, could you?"

"I won't let you steal everything I've worked so hard for! This is my home!"

Lowering the gun, Ray let out a small laugh. "No, you won't." He looked over at his men. "Take her and the boy to the barn and tie 'em up."

Two men grabbed Shell under her arms and picked her up. She tried to shake them off, but they were too strong for her.

"Let me go!"

The men ignored her protests. One of them pulled some rope from a bag and tied her arms behind her back.

"You bastard!" Shell yelled at Ray.

Ray rolled his eyes. "Shut her up while you're at it, please."

Shell was about to scream when her mouth was filled with a disgusting taste. It tasted like she was eating dirt as one of the men shoved a sock into her mouth. She tried to fight the men off again, but it was useless.

They dragged her across the yard where another member of the gang was standing with the boy. They'd tied his arms up, as well.

Shell struggled all the way to the barn, but it was futile. The men shoved her and the boy inside, sending them both to the ground. They slammed the doors behind them and leaving Shell and the young boy in the dark.

"If you ever want out, I recommend keeping your damn mouth shut!"

Hyperventilating, Shell screamed a muffled cry into the sock as the men walked away.

6

SHELL STARED through the cracks in the barn doors as all but one of the men walked away. She heard them all laughing and exchanging high-fives.

"Look at this place, boys! And it's all ours!"

The remaining man stood in front of the door, seemingly to make sure Shell and the boy didn't try to escape.

Shell spit the sock out of her mouth, then turned to the boy who sat beside her. It was too dark for her to see his face, but she knew he was still sitting next to her.

"Everything's going to be okay."

Even in a desperate situation such as this, the boy still refused to talk.

"Are you all right? How's your leg?"

Still, the boy said nothing. Shell held in her frustration.

He's fine. He's breathing, and that's all that matters. If he were hurt, he wouldn't be able to help but make noise.

Shell pulled her hands apart, but the rope held them in place. The man had known what he was doing and bound her wrists with a good knot. She wasn't going to be able to break out of it.

There has to be another way.

"Hey, Sean, come over here for a minute. They aren't coming out of that barn any time soon."

Shell looked through the cracks in the door again and saw the man who'd been standing outside step away from the barn and go toward the house.

This is my chance.

Her mind shifted to cutting the ropes. If she wouldn't be able to pull out of the knot, maybe she could find something inside the barn that would be sharp enough to cut them.

Shell looked around the dark space, picturing what all was inside. She remembered she had left her ax lying in the corner.

"I think I might be able to get us out," she said to the boy. "Stay here and don't move."

Shell managed to get to her feet, though it was difficult without being able to use her hands. She'd made it halfway to the rear corner of the barn when she heard laughing outside. Shell paused. But the laughter was far away, close to the house.

They aren't coming back here right now. They're too occupied with the house. Just keep moving and try to get out of here.

The back corner of the barn was even darker than the rest of the space, making it that much more difficult to see. Luckily, Shell knew every inch of the barn like the back of her hand. She turned around and slid across the wall, moving her hands around to search for the tool. When she was almost all the way in the corner, she found the handle.

"Got it," she said to herself, smiling.

The smile quickly disappeared when she thought about how she would use the ax to break free. The ropes were thick. How was she going to get enough leverage to cut through them?

She moved the ax into the corner where the walls met so that it wouldn't shift around. Then she sat down in front of it. Being careful not to cut herself, Shell sat down and found the ax's blade. She ran the ropes up against the edge and moved her hands up and down. But each time she pressed down, the ax moved. After only a couple of times applying pressure, the ax fell over. On the way down, the handle hit a metal bucket, making too much noise.

Sweat flooded Shell's brow. She got to her feet, balancing on her weak knees, and hurried back over to where the men had placed her.

They're going to know I tried to cut my ropes, and they're going to kill us. I know it.

In the crack under the doors, Shell saw two feet appear outside. She took deep breaths, trying to calm herself, but it was useless. She would lie and say something fell over, but they wouldn't believe her. Furthermore, they wouldn't be able to trust her. And why would they waste time having one of the men look after her and the boy when they could just kill them?

She closed her eyes and thought of everyone she'd lost. It seemed as if she was going to finally get her wish and see them again, though it would be much sooner than she'd anticipated.

"What the fuck?" someone called out.

Then there was a scream.

"Shit!" another man said.

Another scream came, and this time Shell also heard the sound of someone being hit with something.

Shell jumped to her feet then.

"Come on," she said to the boy. "We need to hide."

Though the boy didn't respond vocally, he followed Shell's instructions. They were heading for the back of the barn when a bullet came through the barn door, leaving a hole which allowed some light to shine through.

"Get down!" Shell said, diving to the ground.

She felt vulnerable, unable to cover her head as the fighting outside continued. Men screamed and cursed along with it.

Then, finally, all was silent. The fighting stopped, and all Shell could hear were the breaths of her and the boy, as well as the goats panicking.

Heavy footsteps marched across the dirt outside of the barn. The sun stopped coming from the bullet hole in the door as it was covered by a figure who'd approached the barn.

The barn doors creaked as they opened, and a silhouette appeared in the doorway. Shell squinted her eyes, trying to see the man, but the sun cast a shadow of him. She could tell from his trench coat and shoulder-length hair under a cowboy hat that he wasn't one of the men who'd been with the gang. He held a sword in one of his hands.

The man said nothing as he walked into the barn. He stopped when he made it halfway over to Shell and the boy.

"We weren't with those men," Shell said. "They trapped us in here. Please, just let us go."

Without replying, the man moved closer to her and raised his sword. Shell shook, retreating backward.

"Please," she said. "I promise we will just leave if you'll let us go."

The man walked behind her, and Shell tried to turn so that she'd remain facing him.

"Stay still," he said in a gruff, demanding voice.

She felt the blade cutting through the rope, and then her hands were free. Shell massaged her wrists as she looked at the man. He went to the boy and cut the ropes off of him, as well.

"Thank you," Shell said.

The man didn't respond as he returned his sword to the sheathe. He only glanced at her, and for the first time, Shell got a good look at his face. His beard had more salt than pepper, and he had a scar under one of his slate blue eyes.

He didn't smile once as he turned around and walked out of the barn.

7

SHELL USED her hand as a visor to shield her eyes as she walked out of the barn. But nothing could keep her from seeing the scene before her.

Three bodies lay in the yard in pools of their own blood, still and lifeless. Another hung limply over the banister on the front porch. A fifth man sat against the side of the house, slumped over with his white shirt stained crimson.

Everyone was dead.

Everyone except the mysterious long-haired man in the duster.

And then she noticed someone else was missing.

"Where is the leader? The guy with the stringy black hair. His name was Ray."

The drifter turned around without saying a word and walked away. He headed for the road.

"Wait a minute." Shell jogged after him.

The man continued walking and didn't turn around. Shell reached out to grab his arm but only found the empty sleeve of his coat. Turning around, he grabbed her by the wrist, startling her.

Shell looked into his angry, bright eyes, then down to his hand holding onto her still sore wrist. Her eyes went to the other sleeve of his coat then, and she noticed there was no hand protruding from it. She looked back up at him and he let her go without saying anything. He turned around and started away again.

"You didn't answer my question. What happened to the guy with the black hair?"

"He got away on the one horse that didn't run when the fight started."

Shell narrowed her eyes. She caught up with him again and stood in front of him, blocking his path.

"You can't just leave. I haven't even had the chance to thank you yet."

"No need. Now please, move."

Shell stayed put, crossing her arms. The man sighed and altered his path to walk around her. Shell slid over, blocking him each time he tried.

"Get out of my way, girl."

"No. You think I'm just going to let you leave after all this?"

"Yes. And I suggest you do the same before they come back here." He walked past her, this time pushing her out of the way as he walked by.

"I'm not leaving here. I can't. This is my home."

"That's on you then."

Still frustrated and unsatisfied, Shell caught up with him again. Like before, she stood in his path. This time, he let out a heavier sigh. Before he could speak, Shell cut in.

"I'm not going to let you leave until you let me thank you."

"You already did. Now move."

"That's not how I thank people. Especially for doing the

kind of thing you did. Let me at least get you some food and let you rest here for a while."

"I don't need it."

"What are you going to eat out there? It doesn't look like you have anything on you to put in your belly. And you look like you need rest to me."

"I manage."

"Yeah, well, for once, why don't you let someone treat you? You might as well because I'm just going to keep stepping in your way until you agree."

"Maybe I'll do to you what I did to them."

Shell scoffed. "I don't think you would have let me out of the barn just to do that."

"If I'd known you were going to annoy the piss out of me, then I might have left you in there."

"Come on. I've got fresh vegetables, eggs, even goat's milk. I know you're not going to eat like that if you hit the highway again."

The man looked past Shell to the road. He glanced up to the sky next, checking where the sun sat. Then he shook his head and turned around toward the house.

Shell smiled. "Good choice. I promise that you won't regret it."

It was like watching pigs eat. Literally.

And Shell knew how pigs ate. Up until eight months ago, she'd had three of them. They had, unfortunately, gotten sick and died only a couple of weeks after first showing symptoms.

Now, the one-armed man and the boy tore into the

dinner she'd prepared for them in a way that reminded her of the deceased animals.

Shell bit into a carrot, unsure whether she should interrupt the scene by talking. She finally decided to sit back and let them devour their food. Later, she could try talking to him.

Even from inside the kitchen, Shell could hear the flies buzzing around the corpses outside. She didn't look forward to digging the graves, but it was the only thing she could think to do to dispose of the bodies. They had already started to leave a stench in the air, and she couldn't imagine burning them. The smell and the fire would surely draw attention, too, if any other bandits or gangs were nearby, and could also attract the attention of Deads in the area.

For now, Shell didn't want to think about it. She looked at the boy's nearly clear plate and smiled.

"I guess you were pretty hungry, huh?"

As she'd expected, no response came.

"We'll have to change your bandages here in a little bit. I want to look at those cuts and make sure they're not infected."

When the boy again failed to respond, Shell turned her attention to the man. Though his plate was now empty, he still avoided Shell's gaze. He didn't want to talk, but Shell had so many questions for him. He'd taken out five bandits on his own without garnering even a scratch. What kind of man could do that?

She took a bite of some lettuce, then decided to speak.

"You never told me your name."

Following the lead of the boy, the man didn't respond.

"My name's Shell. Shell Langford."

The man leaned back in the chair and looked in her

direction. He still refused to make eye contact with her, though.

"Look, I'm not doing this," he said.

"Doing what? Talking?"

"There's no point in making small talk and pretending like we're going to be friends."

"Excuse me for wanting to talk. I've been here alone for years, and then all of a sudden, in a day's time, I have almost a dozen people just stop on by."

"Well, lucky for you, I'm not staying here."

"Why?" Shell shook her head. "I don't get it. I saw what you did to those men. Why can't you do that same thing to the others if they show back up?"

"Why would I want to do that?"

"There's a whole town here. It's all empty. Everything we need to survive is right here. I've got plenty of food, loads of medical supplies, and a well with clean water. Do you have a family? They could come live with you here, too."

"Sorry, but I'm not interested."

"Why not? I'd help you fight, too. I'm a pretty decent shot with a bow."

The man smirked. "Yeah? You think you could take down a couple dozen bandits?"

Shell swallowed, her eyes widening. The man nodded.

"That's what I thought," he said.

"How do you know there's that many of them?"

"Because I came across their camp. Part of the group broke off and I followed them here." He took a sip of water. "But the others will come, and there's too many of them. And, besides, I'm not interested in staying."

"Where could you possibly have to go that's better than here?" Shell asked.

He slammed his glass down onto the table and stood.

Shell startled as the man headed out of the kitchen. When the man got to the doorway of the kitchen, he turned around.

"That gang is stationed nearly a day's ride from here, so I'm going to take you up on resting here tonight. But I'm leaving bright and early before they come back in stronger numbers. And if I were you, I'd consider doing the same."

He made his way up the stairs to the room Shell had told him he could stay in.

Shell pushed her plate away. She was no longer hungry.

Her attention turned to the boy, who'd sat in silence as her and the drifter went back and forth. She sighed and stood.

"Come on. Let's get your bandage changed so you can get some rest."

8

THE FOLLOWING MORNING, with the sun pouring in through the window at the end of the hall, Shell approached the door to the room she'd allowed the stranger to stay in. The last person who'd stayed in the room had been Kim, a widow who'd once lived a mile down the road. Her house had burned down, taking her husband with it. Kim had been one of the last people to fall to the sickness which had left Shell as the lone survivor in her town.

Shell had spent the majority of the previous afternoon tending to her animals and sitting in her special tree with her back facing the corpses lying around in the grass. The boy, apparently exhausted, had fallen asleep before the sun had gone down and she never saw or heard him come out of his room by the time she went to sleep. The drifter had remained in his room as well, even refusing to come downstairs and have dinner with her. It had given her time to think about what she was going to do.

The door moved when she knocked. The stranger hadn't shut it all the way. Shell started to walk away to give him some privacy, but accidentally glanced through the crack in the door. The drifter lay on his back with his eyes closed and with no covers on top of him. His pants were still on, but he'd taken his shirt off. Not even the dirt could cover up the scars on his chest and stomach. And for the first time she could also see the nub left where his arm had once been.

One scar, in particular, had caught Shell's attention. It stretched down his left side and had to be eight inches long. It was darker and thicker than most the others.

The scar had pulled her attention away from his face long enough that, when she looked up at him again, the drifter's eyes were open, and he was staring at her.

"I'm so sorry. I was just seeing if you were awake. Whenever you're ready, come downstairs. I've got some food ready." Shell left the room, shutting the door behind her.

If he responded to her, Shell didn't hear it. She turned and rushed down the stairs, nervously pushing her hair out of her face.

"You're an idiot, Shell. That was so creepy."

She was embarrassed, but she'd have to deal with it.

When she got downstairs, the boy was sitting at the kitchen table. He looked at her with the same expressionless face he'd had since they'd first met. She hadn't seen or heard him leave his room.

"You're quite the sneaky one," Shell said. "I don't think I have to ask how you slept. You were out before the sun even went down." She waited for any kind of response, verbally or in his expression, but there wasn't one. "Well, go ahead and eat and then I can take a look at your wounds and change your bandages."

Shell didn't have to tell the boy twice. He scarfed down his food while Shell stared at the stairs, waiting for the drifter to come down. She had so many questions for him, and every scar she had seen on him represented another mystery. The boy burped, pulling her gaze away from the stairs.

The boy covered his mouth, his eyes wide and his cheeks flush. Shell laughed.

"I guess you were hungry. How about we change those bandages now?"

The boy turned toward her, and Shell kneeled down next to him. She uncovered the wounds. They had scabbed over and weren't bleeding.

"They're looking much better."

She dressed the cuts with fresh bandages, then stood and crossed her arms. "Good to go."

The stairs creaked then, and the drifter appeared in the kitchen, wearing a worn gray shirt but not his trench coat; that hung over his arm.

"I've got some eggs and a potato for you," Shell said, trying to put the awkward scene upstairs out of her mind.

The stranger glanced around the room. His eyes fell upon a backpack sitting next to the front door.

"What's that about?" he asked.

"That's what I'm taking with me when we leave."

The stranger looked at her and narrowed his eyes.

"*We*?"

"Yeah." Shell placed a plate with eggs and a potato on it down in front of an empty seat. "Me and the boy are coming with you."

"The hell you are," the stranger said.

"What are you talking about? You said last night that we should leave with you."

"I never said you needed to leave *with* me. I'm not dragging some girl and injured boy around."

"Oh? So, you'll just leave us on our own to figure things out?"

"You seem to have done well on your own so far."

"I *can* survive on my own. But we stand a better chance of staying alive if we stay together."

"I'd question that assumption," the stranger said. "I've done just fine on my own for quite a long time now. I don't need you two slowing me down."

"Fine. You know, whatever. I've lived here my whole life, but I guess I'll figure out where we should go. The highways must lead somewhere, and I guess it'll just mean more food for me and the boy."

"You can't just wander down the highways," the drifter said. "That's where all the road warriors and bandits roam. You've got to know how to navigate them. You're better off dealing with Empties than you are gangs."

Shell raised her brow. "What the hell is an Empty?"

The stranger hesitated, but finally sighed. "Look, I'm heading east. The next city is Jackson, and it's about a two day walk from here. I'll get you there, and then you're on your own. Got it?"

Shell nodded and smiled.

"And, in exchange, I want a quarter of the food and supplies you have to bring along."

"That seems fair enough. Figured you'd ask for half."

The drifter shook his head. Then he sat down at the table and dug into his food.

Shell grabbed her plate and sat at the table for what would most likely be one last meal in her home.

"Dylan."

Shell raised her head from her plate and glanced over at the drifter. her brow creased.

"Dylan Farmer," the drifter said. "That's my name."

Shell smiled then. She wiped her mouth and cleared her throat.

"Nice to meet you, Dylan."

Dylan nodded. "Now let's finish up so we can get out of here."

9

PAUL ROWLAND WASN'T GOING to die today.

He stood with his back flush against the wall, gripping the knife tightly in his hand. Looking out onto the street, he could see the machete he'd dropped. It was only about ten yards away, but the Demons lumbered near it and there was no way he could get to his weapon with them gathered around it. Especially not with only a hunting knife in his possession.

Shifting his focus across the street, Paul signaled to his second-in-command, Keon Jennings. Paul held up five fingers and then four, alerting Keon that there were nine Demons present in the street. Keon nodded, then passed the information to the other two in their squad.

Using other hand signals, Paul directed Keon to head around the building and arrive at the back of the horde. He hoped the others could garner the horde's attention while he ran into the street and retrieved his machete.

Again, Keon nodded, and then he headed down the alley with his younger sister, Katrina. The other member of their convoy, Caleb, remained in his pre-established position, ready to provide Paul cover fire with a crossbow while Paul ran to get his machete.

Closing his eyes, Paul drew in deep breaths. His thick, sandy blonde hair padded the back of his head resting against the concrete wall. He focused his ears, listening for Keon and Katrina to arrive in their position behind the group of Demons. Paul's eyes opened again only when he heard a whistle.

The Demons stopped moving moments later, and Paul heard the first arrow soar through the air. One of the creatures screamed, its body tumbling to the ground not even a second later.

"Go!" Caleb yelled, jumping out from behind the wall and aiming his crossbow at the distracted creatures.

Paul exhaled and threw himself out into the street. He stayed low, looking to avoid any possible friendly fire. Approaching, he watched Keon shift his crossbow around to his back and pull out his own machete, opting to use that on the creatures instead of risking firing his crossbow toward Paul.

Regardless of the distractions, one of the Demons focused its attention on Paul and it moved toward him. The creature blocked his path to the machete. But as he worked to try and find a way around it, the monster suddenly fell, an arrow entering the side of its head above the ear. Paul looked over to see Caleb with his crossbow raised. He lowered it and gestured to his leader to make a run for the weapon as he reloaded.

Paul eyed the machete lying near the remaining Demons. He exhaled again and made a run for it.

The noise he made grabbed the attention of two of the Demons. They turned toward him and snarled just as he reached the machete. Paul rolled over the ground, landing in a kneel as he took hold of the weapon. Even as his hands gripped its handle, one of the creatures lunged toward him. He raised the machete, jamming the blade into the creature's neck and up through its head, destroying it. But the Demon fell on top of him before he was able to withdraw the blade, landing lengthwise above him and pinning him to the pavement.

The weight was too much for Paul to bear. Then as he tried to push the Demon off of him, the second one fell on top of it, only adding to the weight on top of Paul.

The Demon snapped its jaws and clawed with its hands but couldn't seem to figure out how to reach him. The only thing keeping it from getting to Paul was the dead creature sandwiched between them. Paul gritted his teeth, stuck at the bottom of the Demon pile. The creature moved its head over its fallen counterpart's shoulder, its jaws snapping only inches from Paul's face now. Drool dripped down onto Paul's face as he continued to push upward, trying to lift the weight from his body.

Then Paul heard the whistle fly by his ear, and blood splattered down over his face as the second attacking Demon fell limp. He'd closed his eyes, turning away and trying to shield himself from the blood, and when he looked back up, he saw the arrow which had entered the creature's skull, the sharp tip coming out the other end. A shadow passed over Paul, a figure standing above him. Keon.

"Need some help?"

Paul sighed, dropping his head back to the pavement. "Get these fuckers off me."

Keon laughed before kneeling down and rolling the first body off of Paul, then the next.

Paul grunted as he sat up, feeling every one of the forty-four years he'd been alive in his sore back. Keon offered his hand and pulled Paul up to his feet.

"You're welcome," Keon said.

"You mean, 'you're welcome, sir'?"

"Ha! Fuck you."

Paul smiled and extended his hand, which Keon slapped and then shook.

"The area's clear," Katrina said to Paul, coming up from behind them.

"Thank you, Katrina. You can be so much nicer than your older brother."

"Damn straight," Katrina replied. She was five years younger than Keon. Half-siblings, they shared the same mother.

Paul said to them, "Let's salvage all the ammo we can from these bastards and then see if we can secure that hotel."

As the others worked to pull their arrows from the bodies of the fallen Demons, Paul stared up at the King Edward Hotel. It was one of the tallest buildings in downtown Jackson, Mississippi. He only hoped it was empty so that they could make camp there for a few days and scour the city for supplies.

"We're ready to go," Keon said.

"All right, let's go see what this place is all about."

10

"Stay alert, everyone," Paul said as the group crossed the threshold of the hotel's lobby. Some light poured into the space, but the group was forced to creep into a building concealed mostly in darkness. Staircases spiraled up on either side of them, leading to a balcony above the ground floor. The front desk was all the way at the far end of the room, directly in front of them. Between the group and the counter, a chandelier had fallen, shattering in pieces on the neglected floor.

From a dark corner ahead, Demons snarled at them.

"Well, that answers whether this place is vacant," Caleb said.

They moved across the room, each with a weapon in hand. Paul was glad to have the machete back in his possession and he kept his hands gripped firmly around the handle.

Stepping around the fallen light fixture and the debris, they arrived at the front desk. Three Demons roamed nearby in an area too dark to aim crossbows.

"Keon and I will handle them," Paul said.

Spinning the machete at his side, Keon smiled as he headed toward the creatures. "Come 'ere, motherfucker." This drew the attention of two of the monsters.

Paul reared back his machete and decapitated the Demon nearest him.

Then Keon spun his machete again, continuing to taunt the other creatures. He waved them toward him, one of the creatures snarling and lunging at him. Keon jumped back and laughed.

"Quit messing around, Keon," his sister said.

Tired of his friend's antics himself, Paul took out the second beast following Keon, striking it down with his machete.

"Fuck it." Keon finally stopped messing around and raised his machete, driving it into the Demon's forehead. The creature fell, taking the machete with it. It hit the ground, the back of its skull banging off the tile floor with a loud crunch. Keon stepped on the Demon's chest and yanked the machete out of its flesh.

He spun the machete again before jamming it back into the holster he wore on his belt. Not amused, Paul pushed past his friend, bumping shoulders with him.

"What, man?"

"There's no time for you to be messing around like that. We have a job to do. We've gotta check this place out before we run out of sunlight."

Keon shrugged. "I know, man."

"Then quit fucking around and let's get to it." Paul turned around, catching a glance of Katrina shaking her head at her older brother.

"Should we stay together or split up?" Caleb asked.

"Let's split into pairs and search this floor." Paul looked at Katrina. "I'll take Trina with me. We'll head this way toward the restaurant. You and Keon check the offices."

Caleb nodded and signaled Keon to follow him. Paul avoided Keon's gaze as he passed by him. Instead, he merely nodded toward Katrina, and they headed toward the restaurant.

When they had moved into the other room, Katrina said to Paul, "Sorry about that back there."

"About what?"

"Keon being an asshole."

"And that's your fault? I've been around him long enough and I know how he can be."

"Yeah, I know. It's still frustrating."

"I'm just glad he's not my brother." Paul smiled at her.

The two shared a laugh as they made their way into the large dining hall. It was quiet.

"The place seems really empty," Katrina said.

"Maybe too empty."

"What do you mean?"

"If there was anything worthwhile here before, I'm sure someone else who came through here already took it. We're running too low on supplies in our camp."

"This is a big city, Paul. Don't give up hope yet. We can use this building as our base camp and do some scavenging. There's plenty of places around here to look."

Paul wasn't so hopeful. Their group had traveled a long way since leaving Georgia. They'd suffered losses along the way, and he knew they needed to find medical supplies and food soon.

They spent the next hour scoping out the twelve-story hotel, including going up through the first few floors. They didn't find anything useful, which wasn't a surprise. But they also didn't come across any other Demons, nor find any people living there. When Paul and Katrina went back to the lobby, Keon and Caleb were already there.

"Anything?" Paul asked.

Keon shook his head. "Ain't nobody here. And we didn't find shit for food, first aid, or weapons."

"All right, well, we still need to check the rest of it, but it looks like we might have a good place here," Paul said. "This building will make a good base camp, and we can spend the next week or so looking through nearby buildings. Then we'll move on and keep heading west."

They walked outside, and Paul looked up at the sun.

"Still got a few hours of daylight left," Keon said.

"Yeah, we need to go ahead and get the others back here." Paul looked at Katrina and Caleb. "I want you two to go back and lead the others here. Head back the same way we came since we know it's safe. You should have plenty of time to make it the two miles back to camp and then return here before the sun goes down."

"Yeah, we'll see if this fat ass here can keep up with me on the way back." Katrina laughed as she patted Caleb's stomach.

"Fuck you," Caleb said, smiling. He was maybe a little overweight by the day's standards, but the jab was Katrina's way of keeping things loose more than anything else.

Paul laughed and shook his head. "Look, you two idiots just get back here safe with everyone, all right? I'd like to see my wife tonight."

"Don't worry, we will," Katrina said. She hit Caleb on the arm. "Come on, Tubby. Let's move."

They jogged away from the hotel and headed back

toward camp. Paul and Keon watched until they turned the corner and moved out of sight.

Then, Paul put his hand on Keon's shoulder and the two went back inside the building to look around some more.

11

WITH DUSK APPROACHING, Dylan stopped. Shell looked off into a nearby field to see a barn, dilapidated and barely standing. Dylan pointed toward it.

"We'll stay there for the evening."

"That place looks like it could collapse any minute now."

"It'll be fine."

"Why don't we keep going?"

He looked at her, his hat lowered over his face to where she could barely see his eyes. "Because I don't travel at night when I don't have to." He started down the dirt path that led to the barn, and Shell and the boy followed.

When they got close to the barn, Dylan held up his hand. Something inside banged on the doors so hard that they shook, their hinges squeaking.

"I can't sleep here with those things banging on that door," Shell said.

Without replying, Dylan drew his sword from his hip, the steel leaving its sheath with a hiss. He opened the doors and two Deads spilled out onto the ground. Startled, Shell jumped back. But the Deads didn't faze Dylan. He stabbed the sword into each of their heads, then focused on the others exiting the barn. Four more Deads were lumbering into the light. Shell grabbed her bow, ready to use it.

But it proved to be unnecessary.

It took less than a minute for Dylan to slay the Deads. He wielded the sword with masterly precision, all with only one hand. His skill stunned Shell, and all she could do was look on with a slack jaw as each Dead fell.

When it was over, Dylan kneeled down next to one of the fallen creatures. He grabbed its shirt and wiped the blade down with it, then looked at Shell.

"We can sleep here now. I'm going to check the rest of the property and make sure it's clear."

Shell was silent, merely watching the mysterious man as he walked away. She took another look at the Deads lying on the ground and she shook her head. She'd never seen anything like what Dylan had done, and he'd managed it all with only one arm.

Shell came out of her daze and looked down at the boy. He was staring at the Deads, a blank expression on his face. Shell took him by the arm.

"Let's walk around the side of the barn."

Shell led the boy out of sight of the Deads, and they met Dylan who was walking toward them.

"It's clear," Dylan said, returning to them. "There's some wood on the other side of this barn. Enough for us to start a fire. Why don't you both come help me gather some of it?"

Shell and the boy followed Dylan around the other side of the barn to where pieces of the barn lay on the ground, having peeled away from the structure over time. They gathered as much wood as they could into their arms, then headed back to the other side of the barn.

"Thank you for everything you've done for us," Shell said.

Dylan looked at her for a moment, then nodded without saying anything more.

They dropped the wood in the dirt, piling it tightly together. Dylan found a piece of paper lying near the barn and dropped it on top of the stack, as well. Then he took two sticks from the ground and kneeled next to the fire, rubbing them together.

"Oh, hold on," Shell said, reaching into her bag and pulling out a box of matches. "Allow me."

She struck the match and promptly lit the paper on fire. Even without the help of gasoline, the dry wood soon caught. Dylan scoffed.

"You're welcome," Shell said to him.

Dylan then reached into his own bag and pulled out something wrapped in a cloth. When he unwrapped it, he unveiled the remains of a small animal.

Shell coughed and put her arm over her nose. "That's what that smell was."

"I just caught it yesterday," Dylan said. "Along with some of those vegetables you brought, this should make a fine meal."

A grin formed on the boy's face, which managed to push Shell into smiling despite the sight of the dead creature.

Dylan had already skinned and cleaned the animal, and now he cut it into pieces. He found three sticks and distributed the meat evenly before handing one each to Shell and the boy. The moon rose as they sat around the fire, roasting the meat.

Shell had already fetched a jar of carrots and some fresh lettuce from the cart.

"Rabbit with carrots and lettuce," Shell said, thinking of some of the comics she'd read. "A little ironic."

Neither the boy nor Dylan apparently got the joke, and Shell shook her head. She set the vegetables down, and when their rabbit had finished cooking, the three ate.

The boy tore into his food like an animal.

"I know you're hungry, but you don't need to eat so fast," Shell said. "It'll make you sick and you won't feel as full."

They ate in silence after that. Dylan sat on the other side of the fire, his hat covering his face. A gentle breeze blew through their camp, but the air was mostly warm. Shell thought of how relieved she was that winter had passed. If she had been forced away from her home when it had been cold, she couldn't imagine how she would have survived.

When Dylan finished eating, he removed his hat and ran his hand through his long black hair. "I can't remember the last time I had fresh vegetables."

"How long have you been traveling?"

The man hesitated, staring at the inside of his hat. "A long time." He set the hat down beside him. With the glow of the fire illuminating his face, Shell could see the scars on his cheeks that his beard failed to hide. She could also see the wear in his eyes.

Shell swallowed as her eyes went to his missing arm. Dylan caught her gaze and narrowed his eyes.

"How did it happen?" she asked.

"You know, you ask a lot of questions." Dylan looked over at the silent boy. "You should consider being more like him."

Shell bowed her head, moving her bangs from her face. "I'm sorry. It's just that I've been alone for a very long time. It's not often that anyone passes through this small town."

"Get some rest, because we've got a long day ahead of us tomorrow," Dylan said.

With that, Dylan laid down flat on the dirt, using his hat to cover his face. The sword lay under his arm in a position where he could grab it easily in case something, or someone, approached them in the night.

Running her hand through the boy's hair, Shell said, "Rest."

He laid down, curling up into a ball.

Shell did the same, lying on her back and looking up to the stars. She kept her knife and her bow nearby in case she needed them. Having never been away from home, her eyes remained wide open. She didn't know how she would sleep outside. All she could think about was a Dead approaching during the night and attacking them. It seemed unsafe for all three of them to sleep. She was about to ask Dylan if one of them should stay up when he let out his first snore. And when she looked at the boy, she saw that he was also breathing heavy, fast asleep.

She sighed, lying back down.

It would be a long night, and she wasn't sure if sleep would find her.

12

PAUL PACED BACK and forth in front of a second story window. The clouds partially blocked the moon and a breeze blew in through the open window, but it wasn't enough to keep the sweat from collecting on his brow.

"You've gotta sit down, man," Keon said.

"They should be here by now. The camp was only like two miles away. It doesn't take that long to get there and back."

"Everything's cool. Trust me."

Paul turned around. "How do you know that for sure?"

"'Cause my sister's a survivor. She ain't gonna let nothing happen to herself, and she sure as hell isn't gonna let anything happen to the others."

Paul turned back to the window and looked outside again. He wanted to believe Keon. And it wasn't that he didn't trust Katrina. If that had been the case, he would have gone back himself to get the others and bring them to the King Edward. He trusted Katrina and Caleb with his life.

But what if something had happened? There'd be no

way for Paul and Keon to know. The others could have run into a pack of Demons or even a gang of raiders.

"Seriously, dude," Keon said. "Just come sit down. You're making me all antsy and shit, standing in front of the window like that."

Paul ran his hands through his hair and took a deep breath.

He's right. You're doing yourself no good by staring out this window.

There was a worn sofa on the other side of the room, and Paul took a seat on it. Dust filled the air in response to his weight and he coughed, covering his face.

"Damn," Keon said. "How long do you think it's been since someone sat in that damn thing?"

"I don't think I want to know."

"A-fuckin'-men to that."

Paul leaned forward with his elbows on his knees and looked at his friend. "I never thanked you for earlier."

"What do you mean?"

"Covering for me out in the street when we were fighting those Demons."

"Ah shit, Rowland, we're way past 'thank yous' and all that. You'd have done the same for me. Hell, you've saved my black ass more times than I can count."

"Well, it's a nice ass."

Both men laughed, but Paul's smile quickly disappeared. He looked towards the window again.

"Seriously, dude," Keon said. "They'll be back soon."

But that wasn't why Paul was looking out the window now.

"How much longer do you think we're gonna have to run, man?" Paul asked.

Keon shrugged. "As long as it takes."

"You'd think by now we'd have found somewhere to settle."

"Demons have been occupying these lands for thirty years. That's a long time to contaminate shit. We'll find somewhere eventually, but we'll just keep heading west until we do."

Paul shook his head. "We should have never had to leave Georgia."

"But we did. It's time that you accept that and quit blaming yourself for what happened."

"I'll feel a lot better when we find a permanent home."

Keon scoffed. "What the hell does 'permanent' mean nowadays, anyway?"

Paul bowed his head.

"I'm sorry, man," Keon said. "But you know what I mean."

Paul shook his head. "I can't raise a child like this. I already have enough guilt bringing one into this world."

"We're going to find a good place to raise your little one. And don't ever feel guilty. You and Brooke are going to make great parents."

"Yeah," Paul said, looking away again.

It had never been his and Brooke's intention to get pregnant. It had just happened. The only birth control left was abstinence. Paul had run out of condoms a long time ago— it had been over five years since he'd even seen one. Since then, he'd just had to be more careful. And, most of the time, he was. Just not that one time.

Paul stood up and started into the hallway, but a noise drew him back over to the window. Keon stood, too.

Through the dark, Paul could see the silhouettes of over a dozen people. A smile spread across his face. He turned and rushed out the door, Keon following him.

It was so dark that Paul nearly fell down the stairs, but he managed to stay on his feet to run out of the lobby and through the open door leading outside.

Katrina and Caleb were at the front of the group. Keon ran to his sister and wrapped his arms around her. She laughed as she hugged him back.

"Damn. It wasn't like we were gone that long."

"What the hell took so long?" Keon asked. "We thought you'd be back before dark."

"We hit a small pack of Demons on the way there and another on the way back. Also thought we'd come across a gang of people on the way and had to hang low for a few. Turns out it was a false alarm. Your boy Caleb here just heard something in his damn head. But we're here now. It's all good."

Paul searched the fourteen person group until he found his wife.

She stood in the back of the crowd and smiled as she made eye contact with him, and then swiped the bangs out of her face as Paul hurried over to her.

He wrapped his arms around her, hugging her tight. Then he cupped her face, kissing her on the lips.

"I missed you, too," she said, letting out a small laugh.

"I was just getting a little worried because it took so long. But I'm so glad you're here. Both of you."

Paul squatted and kissed Brooke's blue dress on her pregnant belly. He then put his hand there and moved it around. By their calculations, she was at a point where the baby could come any day now. Standing, he kissed his wife again.

"So, this place is good?" she asked.

Paul nodded. "Should be for the next few days while we scavenge the area for supplies."

"Well, my legs hurt. You can kiss me more inside." Her grin grew.

He smiled back and kissed her forehead. Then he turned to the others.

"All right, let's go ahead and head in. We'll get some candles lit and show everyone where they're staying."

13

Shell awoke when something hit her in the ribs. She opened her eyes and immediately shielded them from the sun. Through the blotches of her sight clearing, she saw Dylan standing over her.

"Time to go."

Shell sighed. "You didn't have to kick me in my ribs."

"I only nudged you. Now get up."

Shell sat up and rubbed her eyes. Once her vision cleared, she saw that the boy was already awake and standing. The campfire had been extinguished, likely having died down during the night.

"I'll want to try to catch another animal later on," Dylan said. "For now, we can have some of the vegetables for breakfast, but I want to get going. We can eat while we move."

Slowly standing as she tried to wake up, Shell "Yeah, I get it."

When she made it to her feet, Shell stretched. Dylan grabbed her bag off the ground and stuck it into her stomach while her arms were in the air. Shell exhaled, nearly putting out her back from ending her stretch early.

"Really?" Shell took the bag.

"We need to get going." The enigmatic stranger walked to the road.

Shaking her head, Shell threw her backpack over her shoulder and moved next to the boy.

"Did he wake you up like that?"

The boy shook his head.

"Lucky you."

Dylan arrived at the road, and he stared down the highway. He didn't look back, and Shell wondered what was going through his head. She had so many questions about the strange drifter. For now, she shook them off and took the boy by the hand.

"Come on."

They joined Dylan and started the day's journey down the highway. With every step they took under the warm morning sun, Shell was farther away from home than she had ever been. She had always been protected by her father, and then by Lewis later on. Anytime a group had left the town for any reason, Shell had been forbidden to go along. But by the time Lewis had died, Shell had learned all he had known to teach her, and she felt prepared to make it in the world on her own.

"Eleven years."

They had been walking for half an hour when the words from Dylan had broken Shell out of her thoughts. She looked at him with narrowed eyes.

"What?"

"I've just about lost track of time, but I think I've been on my own for about eleven years now."

"That's a long time," Shell said, still trying to pull herself away from thoughts of her family.

The drifter nodded. "I've had companions come and go along the way. But I've mostly been on my own. I prefer it that way."

"I hope you don't mind my asking," Shell said, licking her lips, "but how old were you when the world changed?"

Dylan remained silent for a moment. Shell felt the heat go into her cheeks, knowing she might have crossed a line by asking the question. She was about to apologize when he continued talking.

"I should have died." Dylan looked into the horizon ahead of them. "When everything first happened, I mean." He laughed. "It's strange. I used to have nightmares about it, but I haven't thought about it now in months."

"I'm sorry I asked."

Dylan glanced at her, then stared back out onto the open road. "I was eleven years old. My grandmother lived in Austin, Texas and I had just been visiting her. I was on a flight back to Virginia when The Fall happened."

"A flight? Like an airplane?"

Dylan grinned. "Yeah, I guess you're too young to remember airplanes. But yes, I was on one of those. Many of the passengers had all of a sudden blacked out, and everyone who hadn't started to panic. The crew didn't know how to handle the situation. Soon, all who had fallen rose, and all hell broke loose." Dylan shook his head. "I did all that I knew to do; I got down on the ground and hid under my seat. I cried and cried, but no one heard me. There were too many screams. So many snarls.

"Not long after, the plane started for the ground. I honestly thought I was going to die. I was so young. I didn't want to die. Then a man—he had been sitting nearby on the plane—loaded back into his seat. He saw me on the floor and picked me up. He got me strapped back into my seat. And I closed my eyes as the plane went down.

"Even though I thought I was going to die, I didn't. And neither did the man who saved me. We were the only two survivors."

"Jesus," Shell said. "That's an incredible story."

"Yeah," Dylan said. "I suppose it is."

Shell looked over at the boy. He'd heard Dylan's story, but still didn't speak. Shell took one more glance at Dylan, then looked ahead and spilled into her own story.

"My mother died giving birth to me. I was raised by my father and his best friend, Lewis. I'm only twenty-three, so I was born into this world well after The Fall. Those two men raised me to survive in it.

"Dad died when I was only six. He was out hunting food and was accidentally shot by one of the men who went with him. The guy felt so guilty that, only two weeks later, one of the other people in the town found him hanging in a closet."

Shell lowered her head, choking back tears. When she looked back up, both Dylan and the boy were staring at her. She noticed a hint of sorrow in the drifter's eyes that she hadn't seen before. But he said nothing, instead only waiting for her to continue her story.

"Lewis raised me after that. He taught me how to do everything... grow food, defend myself, start a fire, perform first aid—everything.

"When I was about to turn seventeen, a strange plague hit our town. One by one, the people died. It happened so often that we became numb to burying the bodies. Near the end, we just started burning them. We used a plot of land on the other side of town to keep the stench away."

"And you never got sick?" Dylan asked.

Shell shook her head. "To this day, I don't know how I didn't. Three of us made it through. Well, almost. It was me, Lewis, and this girl who was a few years older than me named Amanda. It had been nearly a month since we'd last burned a body when Amanda got ill. She only lasted a few days before she passed. That left only Lewis and me. But Lewis got sick the next week.

"He fought so hard. He lasted longer than anyone else had previously—three weeks." Shell lowered her head again. "I felt really lonely when my dad died. But it was nothing compared to when Lewis went. Because, at that point, I actually was alone."

Several moments passed before Dylan spoke again. "So, you've been at that house, by yourself, since then?"

Shell nodded as she laughed. "God, it feels like I've been alone forever, and yet it feels like just yesterday that I buried Lewis."

"Time's a strange thing when you're all alone," Dylan said.

Shell nodded in agreement, and then the conversation seized. She stared at the barren highway ahead, and even though Dylan and the boy were walking beside her, Shell couldn't help but feel as if she were all alone again.

14

THE FOLLOWING DAY, as they were continuing down the highway, Shell stared off into a pasture running aside the highway. A trio of Deads lumbered through the tall grass nearly a hundred yards away. In the dead silence, she could hear their faint snarling. The Deads would never catch up, not at the speed they moved and maneuvering through the overgrown grass. But they were still out there, roaming these rural landscapes, and seeing them was a reminder of that.

The highway offered nothing but barren farmlands and pastures, and she wondered what it would be like when they made it to Jackson. She'd heard the stories of cities with tall buildings. Cars racing up and down the roads. People everywhere. And though she knew the population had dwindled and that no one drove vehicles anymore, she'd expected the world away from her isolated town to be something other than just more of the same. Since leaving Yazoo, though, they hadn't even passed through another. It had been nothing but open land with the occasional deteriorated home or farm.

Staring at the Deads in the pasture, she imagined the

pastures once being covered with corn, cotton, and other crops. Machines and people harvesting the fields. A normal world, as Lewis had called it. But this was her normal, seeing the three lifeless figures wandering through the fields.

They'd walked a couple of more miles down the highway when Dylan stopped.

"Let's give our legs a break for a few minutes," Dylan said.

There was a metal railing along the side of the road, and the three of them went over and sat on it. Shell reached into her bag and pulled out a bottle of water and a couple of carrots. She took a small swig of water from the bottle, then offered it to the boy along with one of the carrots. He took the water and tipped it up to his lips.

"Go easy," Shell said. "We have to conserve it. I'll take a look at your injury before we move on, too."

Dylan stood and walked ten feet away before kneeling down and staring at something on the road. Shell went to him.

"What are you doing?"

Dylan stood. "Thought I saw some fresh human tracks. We're on the outskirt of the city limits now. We've got to be more cautious from here on out."

"This isn't exactly what I expected the city to look like."

"Good, because it's not. You'll see what it really looks like soon enough."

Shell went back to the boy and checked his wounds, removing the bandages. They looked much better, but she put new bandages on just to be cautious of infection.

"This should be the last time we have to change it out. At least for a few days."

The boy smiled. It still bothered Shell that he wouldn't talk, but she hoped he would eventually.

"Let's get going," Dylan said.

They started down the highway again. Gray clouds hid some of the sun's rays, making the walk more tolerable as they moved into the afternoon.

It wasn't long before they began seeing the remains of more buildings standing on each side of the highway. The structures became more frequent, and they soon moved onto a different highway.

This road was much wider than she'd ever seen one get, stretching across eight lanes. Rusted bodies of abandoned vehicles lined the sides of the road. Most had been stripped of anything useful and didn't resemble automobiles at all.

Shell looked around, awestruck by all the structures surrounding her.

"So many buildings," she said.

"We're only now just getting into the city. Never been through here, but if I had to guess, I'd say we'll be coming across downtown a few miles down the road. Hopefully, we can get through before nightfall."

Shell had seen the downtowns of cities only in pictures. "We'll see skyscrapers?" she asked.

"Don't get too excited. This place wasn't much less of a shithole than it is now."

"I thought you said you've never been here."

"No offense, but it's Jackson, Mississippi. It barely qualifies as a city."

Shell didn't respond. All of this was a lot to take in, and it was also beginning to settle in that she was never going home.

"Now, while Jackson ain't much, we still gotta be careful," Dylan said. "A lot of the people left in the world have migrated into the cities. And because of that, there's a lot more Empties, too. Keep your eyes and ears peeled."

"All right."

"You able to load that bow pretty fast in case you have to?"

If I can focus and not be so amazed by what I'm seeing.

And she wasn't sure when that amazement would wear off.

15

EVEN THOUGH THERE were all these buildings, something which Shell had never seen, they still represented nothing. In the old world, they had mattered. Each structure had had a purpose, but now they served none. She wondered if there were supplies left in any of them but knew that Dylan wasn't going to stop to find out. There was no guarantee there weren't other people living in them who would attack anyone who tried to impede on their space. And thirty years removed from The Fall, there was unlikely to be anything of any substantial value left anyway.

The wastelands along the highway did offer her questions about what Dylan was looking for. Where was he going, and what did ht expect to find when he got there? If the rest of the world was like this, then what was the point?

She looked up and saw the sun falling in the sky, and the landscape ahead was still filled with buildings.

"Are we going to make it to the other side of the city before it gets dark?"

"That's the plan."

"And what if we don't? What's the big deal if we have to travel some at night? Can't we just get off the main roads?"

"You're really clueless, girl."

"Pardon me for having lived a good, solitary life up until it was ripped away from me yesterday."

"All I mean is that you don't have any experience out in the world. Surviving out here isn't the same as it was in your secluded town."

I was doing quite well on my own before that gang showed up.

They arrived at a still standing bridge and climbed a hill. When they reached the top, Dylan pointed ahead.

"There."

Taller buildings rose into the sky. Shell had seen photographs in books, but none of it compared to seeing these man-made structures in real life.

"That's the heart of the city?" she asked.

Dylan nodded. "Downtowns are always where I run into the most gangs and bandits. Stay alert."

"I will," Shell said, still taken back by the scene in front of her eyes.

Dylan's brow furrowed. "Is this really the first time you've seen buildings like this?"

"I was never allowed to leave Yazoo City. Others would make trips into the city now and then, but it was rare. The population of our town had declined so much that we were able to live off stuff we already had. I've only ever seen anything like this in pictures in books."

Dylan pursed his lips and then looked ahead into the city. "It's a different world out here, that's for sure. Your loved ones were right for keeping you out of it."

"I lived on my own for a long time. I can handle myself, you know."

Looking at Shell again, Dylan shook his head. "I don't doubt that. But you've got to learn what it's like to live out here. Especially if you plan on being responsible for that boy. So, for now, just keep your eyes and ears open."

The downtown area was on their right when they approached it with less than half an hour of sunlight left. Shell did as Dylan asked, keeping her eyes and ears alert for dangers. She kept the boy close to her as well, periodically looking down at him. His expression was mostly blank as he looked around the ruined city.

Snarls sounded from nearby, but there were no Deads in their path on the highway. They were coming from the right, but when Shell looked around, she couldn't locate the creatures.

"Stay alert," Dylan said, his hand gripping the hilt of his sword.

They had made it down the road a few more minutes when six Deads emerged from behind a toppled semi-truck, twenty yards ahead. There were another four on the other side of the concrete barrier which split the highway, bringing the total count to ten. The creatures started towards Shell and the others, moving at their usual slow pace.

"We've got to turn around," Shell said.

"We can't afford to backtrack. We'll lose too much time."

"You want to fight them?"

"We don't have a choice."

"Of course we have a choice. We can turn—"

"No," Dylan said. "That's not what we're going to do. You told me you were good with that bow, so prove it."

He drew his sword and took a few steps toward the creatures. Then he shifted into a fighting stance.

Shell grabbed her bow and arrows then said to the boy, "Stay back."

The boy moved behind the remains of a nearby vehicle, kneeling down and peeking over the trunk to watch Shell and Dylan fight with the Deads.

Shell set her quiver next to her and got down on one knee with the Deads ten yards away now. She drew a single arrow and nocked it, pulling the string back taut. Aiming at one of the Deads, she drew in a deep breath.

The male creature wore no shirt, its pale gray chest and stomach exposed. Its shoulder slumped, and its head was cocked to the side as it stared at her. Even though the Dead looked human, it wasn't—that's what she'd long ago been taught by Lewis. This had been one of his many lessons when he'd taught her archery.

With deep breaths, she recited the words he had said to her when he'd first taught her how to shoot.

"Aim true and vanquish the past. End the pains of a life once lost."

The Dead opened its mouth wide as it snarled. Shell exhaled and let go of the bowstring.

The arrow soared through the air, hitting its target. It pierced the back of the Dead's throat and came out the rear of its head. The creature fell back onto the ground.

Dylan looked back at her, his face not showing he was impressed.

"Hell of a shot. But aim for the brain. Only way you'll take 'em out for good."

She drew another arrow and aimed again. This time, she aimed for the forehead of her target. And, like before, she wouldn't miss.

The arrow entered above the creature's right eye,

spraying blood into the air. The Dead hit the pavement with a thud and Shell drew another arrow.

The creatures had advanced close enough for Dylan to attack. He raised the sword above his head and lunged at one of the Deads, burying the blade in its skull. He had little trouble getting it out, which surprised Shell. She wondered how many times he would get that lucky, especially without a second hand to use as leverage for wedging it back out after a strike. But he'd made it this long by himself, so Shell worried about herself and focused on nocking another arrow.

She was about to exhale and let loose when she heard a screeching snarl come from her right. She looked over to see four more Deads spilling over the concrete barrier, each falling on their faces but unfazed.

"We've got more company!"

Dylan lopped the head off another creature and looked back briefly before one of the other creatures lunged at him. He barely jumped back in time.

"Stay focused," Shell said.

She turned to aim at the new creatures which had come over the barrier, firing an arrow at the nearest one.

She missed.

Damn it.

Her hand shook as she nocked another arrow. She breathed steadily, telling herself that she had to calm down.

She aimed at one of the Deads that had made it over the barrier. It got to its feet as she exhaled and fired. The arrow landed at the top of its forehead, sending the creature back and onto the ground.

"No!"

Shell followed the scream to see Dylan lying on the highway, a Dead lying on top of him. The creature chomped at his face while the drifter struggled to hold it back with his only arm.

Nocking another arrow, Shell left the Deads she'd been fighting and moved to help Dylan. She had the Dead's temple in her sights, but she couldn't fire. Dylan's head was only inches away, and one miscalculation could kill him. He looked over at her, gritting his teeth.

"Shoot!"

Another Dead was down by Dylan's legs, and he kicked to fight the creature off. Shell couldn't delay any longer.

She exhaled, her sights set on the creature trying to bite off Dylan's face. Sweat collected on her brow. Her hands shook slightly. She still couldn't bring herself to let go.

An arrow blew through the Dead's face.

But it hadn't been Shell's arrow.

The whistling of another arrow sounded, blasting the Dead trying to get at Dylan's legs.

Dylan let out a scream and clutched his leg. The second arrow had killed the Dead, but also pinned its head to Dylan's leg in the process.

Shell turned when she heard footsteps. Four people came over the barrier wielding various weapons. They struck down the Deads that Shell had left behind to help Dylan. Near Dylan, a couple of other people took down the remaining Deads surrounding him.

Within seconds, all the creatures were down. A group of six people now surrounded Shell, Dylan, and the boy who had emerged from hiding and come to Shell's side with the Deads now taken down. They all stared at each other.

Shell realized she still held the bow in her hands, an arrow loaded. These men and women had saved them from the Deads, but what did that mean? She suddenly realized they had three bags with food and medical supplied in them. These people would surely want to take them.

But Shell knew she couldn't take them down herself, and Dylan was injured.

She kneeled and put her bow on the ground, then raised her hands into the air. The boy remained behind her, hiding his face.

"Just don't hurt us," she said. "You can take everything."

A black woman wearing black cargo pants and a gray shirt stepped forward.

"We're not those kind of people." She stuck out her hand. "My name's Katrina."

Shell hesitated before shaking her hand.

"You don't want to kill us and take our things?"

She shook her head and smiled. "Not at all."

16

Dylan grimaced, holding his hand over the base of the arrow in his leg. The arrow had gone all the way through the Dead's head and then his leg, its blood-soaked head coming out the other side.

"Jesus," Shell said.

"Where's the bastard that shot me?" Dylan asked.

"You mean the guy you owe thanks to for saving your life?" The black guy stepped forward.

"Chill, Keon," Katrina said.

Keon gestured toward Dylan. "I just saved dude's leg from getting eaten off by a Demon and he don't even give a shit."

"Maybe you should practice shooting more," Dylan said.

"Man, fuck this," Keon said. "Let's just leave these fools here."

"Come on," one of the others, a larger guy, said to Keon. "Let's go cool off." They walked away, climbing back onto the other side of the barrier.

"He's cocky, but you might want to think about being a

little bit nicer to him since he saved you from getting bit," Katrina said.

"I wouldn't be that cocky if I shot like that."

"Cut the crap, Dylan," Shell said. "She's right. Now we've got to get this thing out of you."

"You should hurry," Katrina said. "There could be more Demons around here, and we'll need to get him back to our camp so that we can help him further. We have a nurse there."

"I'm not going with these people anywhere."

"Can you give us a minute?" Shell asked Katrina.

"Sure. But we're not waiting around forever." Katrina joined the others, just out of hearing distance.

"What's your problem?" Shell asked.

"You haven't lived out on the roads."

"What's that even supposed to mean and why does it matter right now?"

"It means that you don't know how to survive out here. You might be able to grow a vegetable garden, and as it turns out, you're pretty decent with that bow, as you claimed. But it's different out on the highways. We can't trust these people."

"That's bullshit. There's a group of them and only three of us. And last time I checked, one of us is an unarmed child, and another has a hole in their leg. I think they could have left with all our stuff by now, and even killed us if they'd wanted."

Dylan rolled his eyes. "You've got too much trust in people."

"And you don't have much of a choice. Because you can't walk, and I've got the stuff we need to fix you up. So if you don't want to go with them, then I'll leave you out here for more of those Deads to find you, or for some nasty people to stumble across you."

Dylan snarled. "Just get this damn thing out of my leg."

"And you're going to go with them?"

"I said, 'whatever.'"

"I'm not doing anything until you say 'yes.'"

"Yes, I'll go. Now get this fucker off me and this arrow out of my leg."

Shell went into her bag and pulled out a towel and a bandage. She laid it out, then Katrina returned.

"You guys decide what you're gonna do?"

"We're going with you, but we've gotta get this arrow out of his leg first. Can you help me?"

"Yeah. We need to hurry so we can get back before it gets too dark."

Shell drew her knife from her waist and cut off Dylan's pants below the knee. Then Reaching down to Dylan's waist, Shell grabbed his belt. Dylan raised his eyebrows at her.

"What the hell are you doing?"

She ignored him, unclasping the belt and pulling it out through the loops. When she had it in her hand, she folded it up and then put it in Dylan's face.

"Open up and bite down on this."

He bit down on the leather belt and closed his eyes.

Shell placed her knee on the bottom part of Dylan's leg for leverage. She broke the back side of the arrow, removing the tail so that only the shaft of the arrow would pass through the wound when she pulled it out. But first she had to get the Dead off of it.

"Here's where I'm going to need your help," Shell said to Katrina.

Katrina shook her head then kneeled down. "Luckily, or maybe unfortunately, I've done worse."

Shell grabbed onto the Dead's shoulder, and Katrina took the other. They looked at each other, and then Shell counted to three.

Here goes nothing.

"Now!"

They pulled simultaneously, and the creature's brains made a wet sound as the head was pulled off of the arrow. The momentum sent Shell onto her back, and when she sat up, she looked at the Dead. She shook off how disgusting it all was as Dylan scooted away from the corpse, groaning as he moved a couple of feet from it.

Shell then moved over next to him.

"Keep biting down."

Dylan lay down on his back now. He bit into the belt before looking up at Shell and nodding, signaling that he was ready.

She grabbed the arrow near the head and pulled. It made the same wet sound as it slid past torn flesh, tissue, and muscle. Dylan clenched his eyes shut hard and banged his hand against the concrete. He kicked the leg Shell wasn't holding down.

Blood came seeping from the wound.

Shell grabbed the towel and held it to his leg, pressing it against both the entrance and exit wounds. She looked over at Katrina.

"Keep pressure so I can wrap it."

Katrina took over the towel for Shell and she grabbed a bottle of alcohol. She unscrewed the cap and leaned toward the leg again.

"Bite down again," she said to Dylan.

Katrina removed the towel and Shell splashed alcohol

over the open wounds as more blood came out. Dylan arched his back and screamed into the towel. When she'd finished cleaning the wounds, Katrina pressed the towel against them again.

Snarls sounded nearby, pulling both Shell and Katrina away from Dylan. More Deads were coming.

"Don't worry," Keon said. "We'll hold 'em off."

"We've got to hurry," Katrina said to Shell.

"We're almost done. Apply more pressure. We need the bleeding to calm before I can wrap it. I've only got so many bandages and I can't waste them."

Dylan spit out the belt. He groaned.

"How are you doing?" Shell asked.

"I'm fine." Dylan gestured to where Keon and the others were fighting off the three new Deads twenty yards away. "Just make sure that asshole doesn't shoot me again."

"I really hope you plan on getting past that shit if we're gonna bring you into our camp," Katrina said.

"He will," Shell said before Dylan could answer with another smartass comment. "Go ahead and pull the towel off so I can wrap it."

Katrina lifted the towel. Dylan was still bleeding, but it had slowed down enough to dress. She wrapped the bandage, pulling it taut on each pass. Dylan groaned, but didn't yell out again. When she was finished, Shell stood.

"The boys are going to have to help him walk," she said.

"I don't need them to carry me," Dylan said. "Just help me to my feet and I can walk."

With that, Katrina took Dylan's hand, and Shell kneeled and lifted up behind his shoulders. Dylan grimaced, having to push himself up with only one leg, but he made it to his feet. Shell put his arm around her for leverage, and she could already tell there was no way he was going to be able to walk.

Keon took out the last Dead with a machete, then he and Caleb rejoined the group.

"You're not going to be able to walk without some help," Shell said to Dylan.

"Bullshit. I'll be fine."

Keon approached Dylan's side with no arm, and he put his arm around him.

"Come on, hoss. Don't try to be a tough guy."

Caleb approached Shell's other side, and he nodded at her. She moved out of the way, and Caleb put Dylan's arm around him.

Dylan snarled, obviously unhappy that the two men were having to carry him. But Shell was happy, knowing it was for the best and that he'd only end up collapsing.

"Our camp is only a half-mile away," Katrina said. "Follow us."

17

"Did you feel it that time?"

Paul laughed and shook his head. Brooke opened her mouth in surprise.

"Are you serious?" she asked. "It's kicking like crazy!"

"Maybe he's kicking the other direction," Paul said. "Maybe I should have my hand on your back."

Brooke slapped him on the arm. "Idiot."

Paul laughed again. "Hey, you shouldn't talk like that. What if he can hear you? You don't want his first word to be 'idiot' or 'asshole,' do you?"

The smile left Brooke's face and she looked away. Confused, Paul took her by the chin and faced her toward him again.

"Hey, what's the matter?"

"You keep saying 'he.' You've been doing it for a couple of weeks now. I haven't said anything, but it's starting to bring me down."

"I'm sorry," Paul said with a slight laugh. "I honestly haven't even thought about it. I guess it's only natural for me to say 'he' and 'him.'"

"Are you going to be sad if it's a girl?"

"What?" Paul's face crunched into a frown. "No, of course not. Why would you think that?"

Brooke shrugged. "I don't know. There's just a lot on my mind with bringing a baby into this world. And it seems like you're really expecting it to be a boy, and that you won't be happy unless it is."

Paul leaned in and cupped his wife's face. He ran a hand through her curly brown hair and looked straight into her blue eyes.

"Baby, I don't care what we have. I'm going to be overjoyed and happy no matter if it's a girl or a boy."

He kissed Brooke on the lips. When he pulled away, she was smiling again. Paul raised an eyebrow.

"Now, if he's black, that might be a different story. I know Keon used to—"

"Oh, stop it," Brooke said, laughing and hitting him on the arm.

Paul also laughed, and he took Brooke's hands into his own, running his fingertips across her palms. He then let go of one of her hands and rubbed her belly, hoping to feel a kick.

"Speaking of whether it's a boy or girl, we haven't talked much about names lately."

Brooke squeezed Paul's hand. "I don't have to think about them. I told you what names I like."

Paul sighed. "I thought we agreed we weren't going to go with either of those."

"*You* said you didn't like those."

"It's not that I don't like them. I just think we can do better."

Brooke shrugged. "Then come up with something better."

"I'm sorry I brought it up," Paul said. "I don't want to fight right now."

"I'm not fighting. I just don't understand why you feel so strongly against 'Jude' for a boy and 'Eloise' for a girl."

Paul had brought up the names conversation to lighten the mood, not to cause more tension. He had to try to remember how difficult this all had to be for Brooke. Few people they knew had brought children into this world, and Brooke had to deal with that reality on top of going through the tribulations of pregnancy. The world might have changed, but a woman's biology hadn't. Paul took a deep breath. He was about to dive into another apology and change the subject when he heard people approaching from outside. He hurried to the window.

The others were back, but they weren't alone. A woman he didn't recognize stood next to Katrina. She was holding the hand of a young boy who had to be under ten years old. And there was a man with long hair and a beard being propped up by Keon and Caleb. The man hobbled on one leg, and the other was wrapped with a crimson soaked bandage.

"Everything okay?" Brooke asked, coming to Paul's side.

"I'm not sure. Look."

"Who are those people?"

"Paul! Brooke!" Katrina shouted. "Get down here, now!"

"Jesus," Paul said. "Why the hell is she yelling?" He hurried to the door and down the stairs, wanting Katrina to stop so she didn't lure any Demons to the building.

He jogged through the lobby and out the front door. By the time he got there, the group was right outside. He put his arms out, wanting answers.

"Why are you shouting?" Paul asked. "Tell me what's going on."

"We'll explain everything later," Keon said. "But we've got to have Brooke have a look at this guy."

The door opened, and Brooke came out holding her stomach. She narrowed her eyes at Paul.

"Thanks for waiting on me," she said, striking a cold glare at her husband. Then she looked at the others. "What's going on?"

The woman Paul didn't recognize said, "He got shot with an arrow. I wrapped it up as best I could, but he's still bleeding pretty bad. They said you're a doctor."

"I am," Brooke said. "Let's get him inside."

Paul went over to help Caleb and Keon carry the man into the hotel. He glanced down at the stranger's leg, seeing the blood seeping through the bandage.

"Did you guys run into some bandits or something? How the hell did this happen?"

"I said I'd tell you later," Keon said.

"You're not going to tell him about how you shot me?" the man asked in a weak voice.

"You serious?" Paul asked, looking at Keon.

"I was saving his ass from a pack of Demons," Keon said sharply, looking at the injured man. "Let's just get this fool inside so Brooke can take care of him."

Inside, some of the others had already set a table up in the lobby. There was plenty of light coming through the large windows at the front of the building for Brooke to be able to see and work on the man. They helped him onto the table, then Brooke approached his side.

"What's your name?" Brooke asked the man on the table.

"His name's Dylan," the woman said before the guy could answer. "And my name's Shell. How can I help?"

"Katrina and I can handle it," Brooke said. "Why don't you go explain to my husband what you're doing here?"

18

SHELL KEPT the boy's hand and they followed the two men outside. They went out to the curb and stood next to the road, several dozen feet from the front of the building. No one else was out there.

"You want to tell me what happened now?" Paul asked Keon.

"Pretty simple. We were out on our scavenging run. We heard a pack of Demons, but we also heard humans. Went to scope it out and saw her, a little boy, and some dude with one arm. So, we decided to help them."

Paul narrowed his eyes at Keon.

"Look, man, I know we're not supposed to do that," Keon said. "But they didn't look like bad people."

"Yeah, but you don't know that for sure." Paul looked at Shell and shrugged. "No offense."

"None taken. You're right. It was a risk to help us, just like it was a risk for us to come here."

Paul sighed. "Yeah, I guess that's true, isn't it?"

"I'd say so," Shell said.

"So, what makes you trust us now?"

She gestured towards Keon. "If he'd wanted to, he and the others could have left us for dead out on the road and fled with all our things. Any bandits or road raiders would have killed us and taken off with our weapons, food, and few medical supplies. Also, I don't think you'd have your wife helping patch him up if you planned just to do away with us."

Paul smiled. "All right, so I guess you've got some good reasons. And I can tell you that you're right. There's a lot of bad people out there, as I'm sure you know. But we aren't them."

"And neither are we."

"What were you guys doing out there anyways?" Keon asked. "Where did you come from?"

"I'd like to know the same from you," Shell said.

Paul raised an eyebrow. "What happened to trust?"

"It's got nothing to do with trust. I've just been talking a lot, and I'd like to hear a little bit about you guys."

"Fair enough," Paul said. "We come from Georgia. We had a settlement out there, but things happened, and now we don't. So, we decided to head west and see what we could find. That's brought us here.

"Only been in Jackson a day. We plan on spending a week or so here, scavenging the area for supplies. Once we're done, we'll move on again."

"What are you looking for? Like, at what point will you stop?"

"Once we find a place to settle that meets our needs," Keon said.

"I don't know how far you've traveled or where you come from, but it's hard to find a place that isn't already occupied or hasn't been trashed by the Demons," Paul said. "We'd like to find somewhere a little off the beaten path. Somewhere

where it'll be harder for bandits to find us, and easy to block off from Demons. And with nearly two dozen folks in our group, it's not exactly easy to impede on an already settled area."

Shell thought about Yazoo City and her house. The place was probably overrun by the gang now. They'd likely be handling the dead bodies and planning their next move. She felt it was unlikely they'd come after her, Dylan, and the boy. Dylan had killed several in their group, but they now had a sustainable place to live. It'd be stupid for them to leave what they now had there for some revenge trip.

"What about you? What were you guys doing out there?" Paul asked.

"Our story isn't much different than yours. The three of us crossed paths not too long ago, and we're just out trying to survive like you."

"Well, we're glad to have you around until your friend recovers," Paul said. "We won't ask you to share your things, but we'd appreciate the same courtesy."

"No, it's fine," Shell said. "We don't have a lot of food left over, but sharing is the least we can do for helping us out on the highway and for your wife helping Dylan out now. Even if Keon here did shoot him." She smiled at him.

Keon grinned back. Then he scratched his head and looked away.

"We appreciate that," Paul said. "With that, I think it's about time we get inside. We don't need to be out here at night. Come on in and we'll show you your room."

19

Paul walked over to the staircase and stopped.

"There's still a couple of rooms left with decent beds in them," Keon said to Shell.

"This place still has the beds in it?" Shell asked.

Paul nodded. "Keon can show you to a room."

"Actually," Keon said to Paul. "I was hoping to have a word with you."

"That's not a problem," Shell said. "I wanna go check on Dylan anyways. You guys take your time."

Keon waited for her to get down the hall before he shut the door behind her.

"What's up?" Paul asked.

"I just wanna make sure we're on the same page with everything."

"What do you mean?"

"I left out a detail when I was telling you about what happened. That Dylan guy, he's one bad dude."

"You didn't shoot him on purpose, did you?"

"No, no. That's not what I mean. Though it might be a good thing that I did if they turn out not to be as trustworthy as I'm hoping. What I mean is that I haven't seen anyone fight like him. He was tearing through those Demons like it was nothing. And all with only one arm."

"That's interesting."

"It wasn't just him, either. The woman—she's one hell of a shot with that bow."

"They could be really useful if we can convince them to hang around with our group."

"And if we can trust them."

"Are you doubting that we can?"

Keon scratched his neck. "She seems humble and legit. The kid, he hasn't said shit. But I don't know about Dylan yet. He doesn't entirely trust us—that much I can tell you, for sure."

Paul put his hand on Keon's shoulder. "Well, just be patient and have faith. Let's not jump to any conclusions."

"I'm not. I just want to be cautious."

"You know we will. Now go ahead and show Shell to her room."

SHELL SMILED as Keon and Paul walked out of the room. She stood at the corner of the hall, leaning against the wall. The boy stood at her side.

"Oh, hey," Keon said.

"How's he doing?" Paul asked, referring to Dylan.

"He's fine. They told me he's sleeping, so I decided not to bother him. But don't worry, I didn't hear anything you guys said."

"It's all good," Paul said, smiling.

"Yeah, it's not like we were talking about you," Keon said. He looked away and exhaled. Shell knew he was lying, and that was okay. They were all still feeling each other out. The men were smart to be cautious, just like she was.

"I hope you were discussing where me and the boy here can lay down and sleep," she said, grinning and breaking the tension.

Paul laughed and slapped Keon on the back. "He's going to show you right now." He then glanced at the boy. "Are you all right, buddy?"

Shell wrapped her arm around the boy and pulled him close. "He's not really much of a talker."

"That's all right."

"Your wife is in the other room, by the way," Shell said. "She wanted me to let you know whenever you came back out."

"Oh, all right, thanks. I'll probably see you in the morning then."

Shell smiled again. "Sounds good."

Paul left for the other room. Keon raised his eyebrows.

"All right, well, I'll show you guys to your room then," Keon said. "Need help with your bag or anything?"

Shell adjusted the shoulder strap of her backpack and let out a small laugh. "No, I got it. Thanks."

"Right this way."

Holding a candle, Keon led them away. They rounded a corner and came to a staircase. Most of the steps were intact, but there were holes in a couple of them.

"Watch your step," Keon said.

"You know, it's almost like you work here or something. Showing me the way, offering to take my bags."

Keon laughed. "What? Can a guy not just be a gentleman?"

"Well, of course. But your lines sound scripted or something."

"It'd be pretty nice to live that kind of life, huh? Have a job. Drive a car home to a house with working lights, air conditioning, a damn refrigerator."

"Plumbing," Shell added.

"Ha! Yeah, that would be heaven."

The walls on either side of the hallway had dozens of holes in them. Exposed wiring stuck out, running down to the floor like vines. Debris covered the ground, dust polluting the air as they stepped over it. Keon stopped in front of a closed room and opened the door.

"Here you are, ma'am."

Shell and the boy entered the room. The condition wasn't much different than that of the hallway. But it had two beds and a couch. That was all Shell cared for. She set her bag down on the sofa.

"Please feel free to call the front desk if you need anything, including room service. Our complimentary breakfast starts at 7:00 a.m. in the bar."

Shell laughed. "Yeah, if only."

Keon grinned. "For real, though, we'll bring you some food up."

"You know, I think we're good. We ate a little earlier, and we don't want to get into y'all's supply."

"Don't be silly. It's no big deal."

"Seriously. We're okay. Right?" Shell looked at the boy and he nodded.

"Cool, cool," Keon said. "Well, if you need anything for real, I'll be down the hall in room 223. And make sure you keep the metal latch out on this door to keep it cracked. I don't trust the locks on these doors with no power running to them. You might want to keep it open, anyway, so it doesn't get too stuffy in here. Ain't no one gonna bother y'all."

"Sounds good. Thank you, guys, for everything."

"It's no problem."

Keon turned around, but Shell said his name again before he could disappear. He turned to face her.

"Give Dylan some time. He'll come around and appreciate what you did for him."

Keon nodded, looking at the ground. He then looked up and smiled.

"Goodnight, Shell."

He walked away, and Shell exhaled. The boy left her side and went to the bed. He laid on it, curling up into a ball.

"That's a great idea," Shell said.

20

PROPPING himself up on his elbow, Paul ran his hand across Brooke's forehead, gently swiping her bangs out of the way. She sighed, and it turned into a yawn as she opened her eyes.

"Good morning, beautiful."

"Hey," Brooke said, her voice faint.

"I have to say that watching you sleep will never get old."

"You know how creepy that sounds, right?"

Paul laughed. "You know what I mean. But I figured I'd wake you before I had to get going."

"I'm glad you did. This child is pushing against my bladder."

Brooke eased herself upright and managed to swing her legs over the side of the bed. She groaned and clutched her stomach.

"Everything all right?" Paul slid over to her side and put his hand on her shoulder.

"Yeah, yeah, I'm fine. I just need to pee and for this little person to move."

"Do you need any help?"

"No, I got it."

Brooke stood and wobbled off to the bathroom. Paul watched her, wishing there was something he could do to make her feel more comfortable. He'd tried his best to be there for her, but the further along she'd moved into the pregnancy, the more independent Brooke had become. It wasn't that she was being distant... it was just that she wanted his help less often. Paul knew his wife was strong and independent, and if this was how she wanted to handle her pregnancy, he'd respect that, and continue to be there for her if she needed him.

By the time Brooke made it out of the bathroom, Paul had put on his jeans and shirt, and was throwing his backpack over his shoulder.

"Do you really have to go?" Brooke asked.

"Yeah, I do."

"But it's just a hunt. Can't Keon take Katrina or Caleb with him?"

"Neither of them is the shot I am. Hell, look what Keon did to Dylan."

Leaning against the wall, Brooke bowed her head. She swiped her bangs away from her face and wouldn't look up at Paul.

"Hey." Paul moved toward her, realizing see she was choking back tears. "What's the matter?"

Brooke looked through a window at the morning sun. "The last couple of days have gotten me worried. You know, with the newcomers getting caught up in a fight with Demons, and Keon and the others having to jump in to save them. All that, combined with the kid coming." She looked at Paul with glassy eyes. "I want you to be around for the long haul."

Paul took both his wife's hands. "You don't have to worry

about that. I'm not going anywhere."

"How can you say that? You don't know what you're going to run into out there. Hell, Dylan is already missing an arm. How do you think that happened?"

"You're jumping to a lot of assumptions."

"Are they *really* that much of a stretch?"

Paul sighed. "Nothing's going to happen to me out there. We're very cautious when we hunt and when we scavenge. I trust Keon with my life, and he feels the same. We aren't going to let anything happen to each other."

Brooke took her hands back and wiped her cheeks. She looked out the window again.

"I'm tired of living like this. I'm tired of running."

Paul took Brooke's hand again and led her to the bed. They sat together on the edge.

"So am I, sweetie. Believe me. It's why we're doing all of this to begin with. This is what we have to do to survive right now. But I can promise you that we're going to find somewhere to call home again soon, and we won't have to do all this stuff. For now, you've just got to trust me and let me do what I need to do to help make that happen. The only thing I care about is finding a stable home for you, me, and the little peanut in there. Somewhere where we can live out the rest of our lives in peace. You got me?"

Tears flooded her eyes as Brooke looked at her husband. Sniffling, she nodded.

Paul wrapped his arm around her and she fell onto his shoulder. He ran his hand through her hair, kissing her on the top of the head.

"I've gotta go now. But I promise I'll be back, and I'll be bringing with me a deer or something for us to cook up. Hopefully, venison is one of your cravings."

"Actually, if you could find some chocolate, *that* would be the best."

Paul laughed. He hadn't seen a chocolate bar in at least fifteen years. He couldn't even remember what the stuff tasted like.

"Don't count on it," he said.

Paul kissed his wife on the top of the head once more, and she looked up to give him one on the lips. He stood up and threw his backpack over his shoulder again.

"I'll see you in a bit. I love you."

"I love you, too."

Paul walked out of the room and saw Katrina standing down the hallway. He headed that way, toward the stairs.

"Everything cool?" she asked.

"Yeah, we're good."

"All right. You and my brother be safe out there."

"We will. And do me a favor. Try to get Brooke out to get some fresh air in a little bit. She probably needs a few minutes on her own but see if you can maybe go for a walk with her or something, just around the building where we know it's safe."

"Will do. Bring back something good to eat."

Paul smiled. "That's the plan." He walked down the stairs.

He headed into the lobby where Keon was already waiting for him. Others were hanging around conversing with one another.

"Damn, there you are," Keon said. "I've been waiting here at least fifteen minutes."

"Oh, stop with that shit," Martin said from the other side of the room. "It's maybe been five minutes."

"Yeah, well, it feels like a lot longer. Besides, you better be nice to me, Martin, or I might not share with you."

Martin flipped Keon off and he laughed.

"Sorry, man. I was just spending a little time with Brooke before we left."

A grin extended across Keon's face. "Oh, yeah. I know what you're sayin'."

"Fuck you. Not like that. Let's just go, all right?"

"Cool, man," Keon said, his smile fading. "Let's go."

"Hey, wait up."

They both turned at the sound of the female voice. Shell stepped off the bottom stair and approached them. She held a bow in her hand and had a quiver of arrows over her shoulder.

"What are you doing?" Paul asked.

"I heard a rumor you two were going hunting this morning. The boy is upstairs playing with some of the other kids. The older lady—Amy I think is her name—is looking after them. So, I thought I'd tag along with you guys."

Paul smiled and shook his head. "You know, that's really nice of you, but you don't have to."

"I want to come. You guys have done a lot for us already, and I want to help out."

"I appreciate that, but Keon and I have done this a bunch. We can handle it ourselves."

Shell raised an eyebrow. "You don't want me to come because you think I'll be in the way."

"I didn't say that."

"You didn't have to." Shell thought of all the times she'd been forced to stay home when Lewis and others had left Yazoo City to go hunt or search for supplies.

Paul sighed. "It's not that I think you'll be in the way. I just don't want to be responsible for someone else, especially someone I don't know, while we go out to do this."

"And you won't be. I can hold my own."

"I gotta say, Paul, that she's right," Keon said. "Girl is one hell of a shot with that bow."

Jesus, Keon.

"Besides," Shell said, "an extra set of hands to carry the kill back won't hurt, right?"

Paul looked at Keon, who shrugged and nodded.

"She's right about that," Martin said. "Just let her go."

Paul exhaled. "Well, let's get going then."

21

THE KING EDWARD sat at the edge of downtown, only a couple of blocks from the Amtrak station. And to the north, beyond the train tracks, the scenery quickly became more rural. It looked more like the landscape Shell was used to. They had walked about a mile, leaving the buildings behind and escaping into trees where they hoped to find animals roaming.

So far, they had yet to come across any animals to hunt. But they'd also not come across any Deads, or as Paul and Keon called them, Demons. Dylan had called them Empties, and Shell didn't know why. She thought she'd maybe ask him about that eventually.

The previous day's clouds had disappeared, leaving the sun with an open path to beat down onto the earth. Shell wiped the sweat from her brow, working to keep it out of her eyes.

"You guys have only been here a couple of days, you said, right?" Shell asked.

Paul nodded.

"Have you guys seen many Demons?"

"When we first got to the King Edward, yeah, we had to clear out a big pack of them," Keon said. "Other than that, only the ones we encountered when we met y'all."

"The population has definitely dwindled," Paul said. "Not just with Demons, either. Been a while since we've seen other people. So, it was a surprise that not only did we find you, but that y'all were nice. Well, so far, at least." He smiled.

Shell lowered her head, letting out a small laugh. She thought again of the gang who had overtaken her town, then looked up and tried to push the thoughts of them aside.

"How far along is your wife?" Shell asked, changing the subject.

Paul licked his lips and looked off into the distance. He hesitated to answer.

"I'm sorry for asking. It's none of my business."

"No, no, it's okay." Paul looked at Shell, trying to assure her with his smile that she hadn't done anything wrong. "It's just not exactly easy to keep track of, you know? But from her calculations, we should be at about thirty-six weeks. So, she could go into labor any day now."

"Wow. Congratulations. You guys must be really excited and anxious."

"Yeah." Paul looked down. "If you want to call it that." He immediately looked up and shook his head. "I'm sorry. It's a really stressful time right now. Thank you. I'm excited, but also worried."

"I can imagine."

"Our group's been through a lot," Keon said. "At one point, we were much bigger, but we've had our share of casualties along the way."

"I'd like to find a good home, not only to raise my child

and keep my wife safe, but for everyone," Paul said. "And I'd hoped to find it sooner. I don't look forward to my wife giving birth in some rundown hotel or out on the damn road somewhere."

"You'll find somewhere. I'm confident in that." But there was little confidence in Shell's voice as she thought of what her home and town looked like now with the gang raiding it.

"We had a nice place," Keon said. "But we lost it."

"A damn fine place," Paul said.

"What happened?" Shell had blurted out the question without thinking about it. She cursed herself. "I'm sorry. That was rude of me."

"No, it's fine," Paul said.

"It was going to come up eventually," Keon said. "Probably best that it's when just the two of us are around."

"It's not a very complicated story anyway," Paul said. "We had what we thought was a foolproof plan to keep the Demons out. All the right procedures, checks and balances at every position. But it turned out not to be good enough. Simply, a gate got left open, and it wasn't caught during the switch of a graveyard shift. Before we knew it, the place was flooded with the creatures. We weren't as prepared as we thought."

"Jesus," Shell said. "I'm so sorry."

"It happened," Keon said. "And there's nothing we can do about it. We lost a lot of people, though."

"Twenty-two," Paul said, glancing at Keon and then at Shell. "Twenty-two people. And it could have been prevented."

Shell looked into Paul's face even as he looked away. It was clearly difficult for him to talk about the incident. Enough so that Shell decided not to prod any further into what had happened.

Keon put his arm out, urging Shell and Paul to stop. He put his finger to his lips as he crouched down in the tall grass. Shell followed his gaze to see a deer only twenty-five yards ahead.

Staying low, they crept behind an abandoned car. With most of its rusted body intact, the three were hidden from the deer.

Keon held his crossbow up in front of his face. He pulled out a bolt and loaded it.

Shell grabbed his wrist. "I got this."

Keon's eyebrows squeezed together. "What? No. I can hit it from here."

"I never said you couldn't. But you gotta trust me, right? Besides, I'm pretty sure I owe you."

"Let her give it a shot," Paul said.

Without giving Keon another opportunity to protest, Shell moved into position next to the front of the car. She got on one knee as she nocked an arrow. Closing an eye, she aimed with the larger of the two deer in her sight. She drew a deep breath.

"Aim true and vanquish the past. End the pains of a life once lost."

She exhaled.

Fired.

The arrow soared through the air, and her target screamed. The arrow had entered its neck and now protruded through the other side.

The other deer took off. Shell's target ran, as well, but it only took about a half-dozen steps before it fell onto its side.

"Damn, that was one hell of a shot," Paul said.

"Told you she could shoot," Keon said.

Shell looked at him and tilted her head. "But you didn't want me to try at this one?"

"It's not that I didn't want you to try, but—"

"I'm messing with you." Shell hit him on the arm. "Let's go take a look at it."

She was the first one to stand and jog over to the animal. Its eyes were wide but empty. Its side was still, not rising or falling. Blood came from the wound still, and she could see the arrowhead stained crimson.

The two men approached from behind her and Keon whistled, impressed by what he saw.

"You're an even better shot than I thought."

"We even now?"

"Yeah, I'd say so."

"You two can figure all that out later," Paul said, kneeling next to the animal. He pulled out a knife. "For now, let's skin this thing and haul the meat back."

22

PAUL SWUNG the sack of deer meat onto his other shoulder, shifting the weight. He felt the relief in the shoulder that had been carrying it and he sighed. His hands had cramped from holding onto the bag, the end twisted shut but not providing a good grip.

"You all right over there?" Keon asked.

"Of course," Paul said. "Why?"

Keon laughed. "You just look like you're struggling a bit, that's all."

"I'm fine."

They'd yielded what they estimated to be around fifty pounds of venison from the deer Shell had killed. Paul had split the meat between his and Keon's large sacks. Though only twenty-five pounds rested in each sack, the sun beating down combined with hunger made the trek back to the hotel especially more difficult for Paul. But he wasn't going to admit that out loud.

They crossed over the train tracks less than a block away from the King Edward. Paul saw three Demons lingering on the tracks, but they were fifty yards or so away and heading in the opposite direction, leaving them as no threat. It was more proof that there were plenty of the creatures around, and that they'd have to be extra careful through the rest of their time in Jackson.

"I can't wait to get this in my belly," Keon said. "I'm so damn hungry."

"Yeah, I've noticed you getting a little thick around the waist there, bud." Paul winked at his friend, who flipped him off, and Shell laughed at both of them.

They crossed over the train tracks and moved within a block of the back of the King Edward. Keon stopped suddenly.

"What is it?" Paul asked.

"Listen close. Do you hear that?"

Several shouts came from near the hotel. Paul dropped the sack of venison and headed that direction in a sprint.

"Paul, wait up!" Keon said.

Paul ignored his friend. He ran down the side of the building as he heard the human voices getting louder. As he rounded the corner to the front of the building, he unsheathed his machete.

He slowed his gait and came to a stop as he saw it was only people from his group outside. From what he could see, there were no Demons or bandits. People stood in a semi-circle watching a scene unfold.

Through the cracks in the crowd, Paul saw the injured Dylan lumbering away from the building. Brooke followed him, trying to speak with him, but the drifter ignored her.

Shell and Keon arrived behind Paul, Shell having picked up the other sack of meat.

"What's going on?" Keon asked.

"Oh, crap," Shell mumbled.

"You really need to stay here for now," Brooke said to Dylan. "You're not ready to leave yet. Please, listen to me."

Dylan turned, standing up straight. He got within only a foot of Brooke and pointed his finger into her face.

"You can't fucking tell me what to do! Leave me the hell alone!"

Paul balled his fist. A tingle raced up his arms and sweat arrived at his pores as his body temperature rose.

"Shit," Keon said from behind him. "Paul, hold up, dude."

Paul stormed through the gathered crowd, never taking his narrowed eyes off of the long-haired drifter. Dylan made eye contact right before Paul grabbed onto the collar of his shirt and pushed him against a nearby wall. He raised the machete up to Dylan's throat.

"I don't know who the fuck you think you are, you piece of shit, but nobody talks to my wife like that."

"Paul, stop," Brooke said.

A grin stretched across Dylan's face. "Nah, man. That's the thing; you *don't* know who I am."

"You don't know me, either. And if you don't think I won't shove this blade right through your God damned throat, then you—"

"Let's see it, Cowboy," Dylan said.

The response caught Paul by surprise. He tilted his head, looking into the drifter's sharp blue eyes. The grin had gone from Dylan's face, replaced by a serious but smug expression.

"Don't fucking test me. I'll do it."

"Then do it."

"Dylan, enough of this," Shell said.

"Yeah, come on, Paul," Keon said.

A painful groan sounded behind Paul then, and the group gasped.

"Brooke!" Katrina said.

At the sound of his wife's name, Paul looked back.

Brooke had fallen to one knee and was clutching her stomach. Paul's eyes went wide as he let go of Dylan and hurried to his wife.

Katrina arrived before him, kneeling behind her and putting her arm around her. Paul dropped his machete and slid in next to her. He cupped her face, absorbing the sweat from her skin as she clenched her eyes shut.

"Baby, what's the matter?"

Brooke opened her eyes and tears ran down her cheeks. She didn't say anything. It was as if she couldn't speak.

"She needs space," Katrina said, glancing around. "Everyone, back up. Go back inside, whatever. But just let us have this space." She looked at Paul. "Go grab a pillow or something so we can lay her down."

Paul shot to his feet. He ran inside and grabbed the first pillow and blanket he saw, which had lain on the ground where someone had been resting in the lobby. A group of nearly a dozen people were still lingering when he arrived back outside, including Dylan.

"You all heard Katrina," he said. "Get out of here."

People scattered, and Paul put the pillow under his wife's head. He looked up to see Dylan still standing near the wall. Shell stood next to him, and she'd put her hand on his shoulder.

"Come on. Let's go inside and talk."

Paul turned his narrowed eyes away from Dylan as he walked away with Shell. He ran his hand through his wife's hair.

"Everything's going to be all right."

23

Shell led Dylan to a large room near the lobby. She waited for the limping man to enter and then slammed the door behind them.

"What the hell was that out there?" Shell asked.

Dylan ignored her. He walked to a chair and sat down, finally turning around to face her. He still said nothing.

"I'm serious. Why were you causing such a mess trying to leave?"

"I told you I wasn't staying here. Our deal was for me to get you and the boy here to Jackson."

"Yeah, but we agreed that you would at least stay until you were feeling better."

Dylan gestured with his hands to his legs. "I made it here, didn't I?"

Shell rolled her eyes. "And what if the boy and I wanted to continue traveling with you? Did you even stop to consider that?"

Dylan narrowed his eyes and stood. "Let me tell you something, and you listen good. You're not doing me any favors by traveling with me. I was doing just fine before you and the boy joined me. I helped you, not the other way around."

"Really? That's how you look at it?"

"I'm sorry about what happened to your house. I really am. But understand two things. One is that you don't owe me anything, even though you might think you do. The other is that I'm not staying here with these people. If you want to, that's fine. But I've got places to be."

"And where is that exactly?"

Dylan exhaled and he veered his eyes away from Shell.

"Oh yeah," Shell said. "I forgot. You're headed 'South-east.' Whatever that means."

"It doesn't matter what it means."

Shell clenched her jaw. "Either way, you're not ready to travel. You could barely make it into this room. That's fine walking around this hotel, but if you run into a pack of Deads or a group of people who aren't as nice as this one, then you're going to be in trouble."

"You don't know what it's like out there. Don't pretend that you do."

"Maybe I don't. And I can't control what you do. But I'm asking you to stay here until you're closer to a hundred percent. Despite how you might feel, I've come to like you, and I don't want you running out there and getting yourself killed."

Dylan exhaled. He glanced around the room, seeming to consider what Shell had said.

"We brought a deer back," Shell said. "Don't tell me you can turn that down."

Looking at her, Dylan raised an eyebrow. Shell's smile grew.

"I thought that might entice you to stay a little longer."

"It doesn't hurt." Dylan ran his hand through his hair. "I'll give my leg a couple of more days. Then, I'm gone."

"Fair enough," Shell said. "But you've got to apologize to Paul."

Dylan's brow creased. "Now you're just pushing it."

Shell crossed her arms and tilted her head to the side.

"Fine," Dylan said with a sigh.

"Good. Now that that's settled, I'm gonna go see if they need help prepping my deer."

"*Your* deer?"

Shell shrugged. "Yeah. I mean, I shot it, after all."

Dylan snorted a laugh and shook his head. Shell smiled, enjoying the rare amusement coming from the drifter.

"I told you I was a good shot with a bow."

"Yeah, I guess you are," Dylan said. "I'm gonna go rest for a while."

"I'll see you at dinner, then. You can wait until then to apologize to Paul."

Dylan raised his eyebrows as he walked past her.

SHELL WALKED over to the boy's bed. He lay on his back, his right cheek against the pillow as he snored. Shell smiled as she watched him sleep. She still had so many questions about where the boy had come from but doubted they would ever get answered. As far as she could tell, the boy physically wasn't able to speak.

She ran her hand through his hair and said, "Hey."

The boy's eyes opened, and he looked up at her.

"Time for dinner. Are you hungry?"

The boy nodded. He rubbed his eyes and sat up.

"There's some food ready downstairs if you're hungry."

The boy's face lit up with a smile.

Shell laughed. "I'll take that as a yes."

He stood up and they exited the room.

The hallway was empty as they made their way down it and on to the stairs. As they got closer, Shell could hear chatter. Everyone had already gathered downstairs for dinner. Shell slid her hair from in front of her face, something she'd always done when she felt nervous. These people had been friendly to her, the boy, and Dylan so far, but she still didn't know them all that well. Now she was heading to a social gathering with them. Considering how long she'd been on her own, it was a strange occurrence for her.

They reached the main level of the hotel and followed the voices to an open room. The faded sign on the wall next to the door read Ryan Hartman Banquet Hall. Shell crossed the threshold.

Around a dozen candles illuminated the space. A large table sat in the middle of the room which was big enough to sit all of the nearly twenty people in the group. There was a separate, smaller table where the three kids sat playing a board game. Some of the adults stood and mingled, but most everyone had found a place at one of the tables and sat awaiting food.

Keon had been talking to a woman at the side of the room when he turned and made eye contact with Shell. He smiled, said something to the woman, and then walked toward Shell.

She smiled back, again swiping hair from her face with her clammy hand.

"Nice to see you down here," Keon said.

"You kidding? You think I was going to miss out on that deer I singlehandedly shot?"

Keon laughed. "You really gonna hold that over my head?"

Shell shrugged, smiling again.

"You know, I would have shot it if you would have given me a chance."

"But what's it say about me that I so easily talked you into letting me do it?"

Keon looked down and shook his head. Then he looked back up at Shell and his smile disappeared. The rest of the room went quiet.

Shell turned around.

Dylan had come limping into the room, his eyes looking at nothing or no one in particular. He then found Shell's gaze.

She wasn't smiling anymore, either. Like everyone else, she was curious about what Dylan would do. Though everyone else in the room thought different, Shell didn't know this man all that well. He was just some stranger who had, for Shell's sake, been at the right place at the right time.

His eyes looked away from Shell and she followed his gaze.

Paul was standing now, his wife still seated in the chair next to him. He was staring at Dylan with anger in his eyes.

Shell looked back at Dylan, who returned the same expression, focused right back at Paul. He made eye contact with Shell again and she shook her head.

Don't do this. Do what's right.

Dylan stared at Paul as he moved past Shell. The room remained silent as he walked up at Paul, stopping only a couple of feet away from him. Keon looked at Shell and shook his head, then stepped over next to Paul.

"You've got a lot of nerve, showing your face around here after what you did earlier," Paul said.

"Come on, man," Keon said, putting his hand on Paul's shoulder. "Let's sit down and eat."

"You crazy? I'm not eating here with this bastard."

"Seriously, Paul," Brooke said. "It's okay."

"No, it's not okay."

The two men stared at each other. Shell breathed slowly, looking back and forth between their faces. Thick tension filled the room. Everyone waited to see who would snap first.

Dylan then looked down at Brooke. She had a hand resting on her bump, and she stared up into his blue eyes.

"I'm sorry about earlier, ma'am," Dylan said. "I appreciate everything you've done for me, and you didn't deserve to be treated like that."

"You're damn right she didn't."

"Paul, shut up," Brooke said.

She groaned as she pushed herself up out of the chair. Paul put his hands on her and asked her to sit back down, but she pushed him away. She stood all the way up, both hands on her stomach now. She then removed one of them and extended it to Dylan.

The drifter glanced down at the woman's hand, then back up into her eyes. Finally, he brought up his hand and shook hers.

Brooke smiled and nodded at Dylan. The two said nothing to each other as their hands separated.

Brooke returned her hand to her stomach and looked around the room. Everyone was still silent and staring at them.

She shrugged and asked, "Are we going to eat, or what?"

24

WHILE THE BOY ate at the kids' table with the three other children, Shell and Dylan broke bread with Paul, Brooke, Keon, Katrina, and Caleb at the end of the larger table. She hadn't spent any time getting to know anyone else in the group, but she was still adjusting to being around other people again.

Shell could still feel some tension between Dylan and Paul, but most of it seemed to have disappeared after Dylan's apology to Brooke. Luckily, Shell had the deer to distract her, but she still wondered who would break the awkward silence first.

She looked around, watching the people at the table eye her and Dylan. She lowered her eyes to her plate, then raised them again when she heard some throat clearing and an under-breath laugh.

"Can you guys believe that Shell here thinks that we wouldn't be eating this if I had been the one to take the shot?" Keon asked.

Brooke put her hand over her mouth, holding her food in as she laughed and looked at Shell. "Wait, you shot this?"

"Yeah, but I don't understand why that's funny."

"No, no, sweetie. It's not funny that you took the deer down."

"We're just a little amazed that you were able to shut down Keon's ego," Caleb clarified.

"Pssh," Keon said. "I don't have no ego."

Now Paul joined in on the laughing, taking a drink of water as the grin spread across his face.

Keon lowered his head and shook it. Katrina patted him on the shoulder.

"We're just fuckin' with you, bro. It's all good."

"You've provided us with plenty of meals," Brooke said.

"I gotta say, though," Paul said, nodding at Shell, "that was one hell of a shot."

"I've had a lot of practice." Shell thought of the first time Lewis let her shoot his bow. They'd used the target on Shell's favorite tree, and she'd been a terrible shot the first time. She lowered her head to her plate, trying to block out the memory for now and focus on getting to know the people here at the table.

"What's the plan for you all here?" Dylan asked.

"The plan for all of us here is to live," Paul said. He leaned back in his chair, staring at Dylan as if he were waiting for him to snap. It was like he wanted him to.

"And how do you plan on doing that?" Dylan asked.

"We're going to keep moving until we find somewhere sustainable," Keon said, answering before Paul could give another short, smartass answer.

"Why head west?" Shell asked.

"Why not?" Keon asked. "It was no good where we were. And the climate gets too frigid up north—we'd never survive." He looked at Dylan. "You were headed east when we found y'all out on the highway."

"That's right."

Paul scoffed. "Good luck with that."

Dylan leaned forward. "What do you mean?"

"I mean there ain't shit out east. The whole damn coast is a wasteland, and there's a whole hell of a lot of Demons out that way."

"How do you know that if you haven't been there?" Shell asked. "You said you were in Georgia the entire time before coming here."

Paul gestured to the others in his group around the table.

"*We* were. But we had others pass through our camp, and even a few join us, who had been out that way."

"They all told us the same thing," Keon said. "Not to go east."

"We even had folks migrate up from Florida," Paul said. "They'd come up from the Tampa area and told us not to bother heading that way."

"I don't know what it is you're looking for by going east, but you're not going to find it," Keon said.

"And what exactly do you hope to find by heading west?" Dylan asked.

"Hope," Brooke said, breaking her silence.

Dylan scoffed. "Hope is bullshit."

"It is if you have no faith."

Dylan stared at the pregnant woman for a moment more with mocking eyes before looking away, clearly not wanting to insult her.

"The weather is a whole hell of a lot better out west," Keon said. "We're not sure if we can survive another summer down here, and it's too dangerous to migrate back and forth between north and south, depending on the season. We want to find somewhere we can sustain in a fair climate."

"It's a lost cause," Dylan said.

"But we're all after something," Brooke said. "Aren't we?"

She was talking to Dylan, staring right at him. His lip quivered a little, and then he stood.

"Thank you for dinner, but if you'll please excuse me."

Dylan left his chair shifted away from the table as he left the room.

Shell wiped her mouth and then pushed her chair back.

"You're leaving?" Keon asked. "Please, stay and eat with us. We don't have to talk about this anymore."

"No, it's quite all right," Shell said. "I'm pretty tired after today anyway. It's probably best if I get some rest. Thank you so much for cooking this, though."

"Thanks for shooting it," Brooke said.

"A hell of a lot more than Keon could have done," Caleb said, smiling.

"Fuck you, Caleb."

Shell grabbed Keon's shoulder. "I'll let you get the next one."

He smiled and nodded as she took her hand away.

She went over to the table where the kids were eating to see if the boy was ready to go back upstairs. She saw the boy smiling and laughing with the other children and decided not to pull him away from that. It was the happiest she had seen him, so she didn't want to disturb that moment. She turned to the rest of the room.

"Goodnight, everyone," she said, and she left the dining hall and headed up to her room.

25

SHELL SHOT upright in the bed, gasping. Sweat trickled down all over her body, feeling like spiders crawling on her skin. She threw the covers off her and swung her legs off the side of the bed.

She looked around the room, noticing the boy in the bed next to her, still fast asleep. She rubbed her forehead, then covered her eyes.

"Jesus Christ."

She'd had the dream again. The one where she'd seen her parents in the front yard of her house. It took her glancing around the room to see she was still inside of the King Edward to realize it had been only that—a dream.

She slid on her pants and sneaked out of the room without waking the boy, moving through the crack in the door.

She walked down the hallway, still being quiet so she didn't wake anyone, and moved down the stairs to peek around the corner. She saw a man on watch in the lobby. She couldn't remember for sure, but she thought his name was Trent. He sat in a chair with a clear view out the front door. Shell wanted to be alone, so she didn't want to get his attention. She walked in the opposite direction and headed to the room they'd had dinner in earlier. The door was cracked, and she opened it and went inside.

It was dark in the room, but Shell had a solution for that. Reaching into her pocket, she pulled out a matchbook. She grabbed one and pulled it out of the package. Using her hand, she found the rough edge, then struck the match on it. The small flame came to life and she cupped her hand around it to keep it going. She guided it to the wick of a candle that had been left behind, and the candle lit. She lit one other candle, then decided that was enough.

The table they'd had dinner at still sat in the middle of the room, mostly cleaned off. She decided she didn't want to sit at the table. Across the room, she saw a bar. Most of the stools were still in place, as they were screwed into the ground. Cabinets on the wall behind it were mostly in tact, but long vacant of bottles of liquor. She made her way over to the bar and sat down.

"Can't sleep, either?"

Shell jumped at the sound of the familiar voice. She looked at the door and watched Keon come into the light.

"Jesus, Keon. You scared the mess out of me."

"Sorry about that."

"How did you know I was in here?"

"You might be a good shot with a bow, but your stealth could use some work. Trent and I both saw you. And apparently, you didn't see me."

Shell grinned, snorting a small laugh. "And here I was thinking I was being sneaky."

"Not quite."

The two shared a laugh.

Keon approached the stool next to her. "Mind if I have a seat?"

"You're here, so I suppose that's all right."

"I can go if you'd prefer." He gestured towards the door.

"No, no. Don't be silly. Sit."

Keon sat down, leaning back in the chair and letting his body hang loose.

"So, you couldn't sleep, either?" Shell asked.

"Nah. I honestly don't sleep a ton these days. I try to get on watch as much as I can, but Paul insists that I at least try to get some rest. Most nights, I end up sneaking down and hanging with whoever is scheduled on guard. It's better to have more than one person doing that job anyway, especially with Trent. I always feel like that dude could fall asleep at any time. What about you? Why are you up?"

"Bad dream."

"Ah, gotcha. I have those now and then. Hard not to, I guess. You know, with the way we're living."

"How long have you been with this group?"

"That's a damn good question. Been a hell of a long time. Seems like forever."

"It's cool if you don't want to talk about it."

"Nah, I don't mind. My sister and I joined up with Paul about ten years ago. For a long time, it was just the four of us —me, Katrina, Paul, and Brooke. But then our community slowly started to grow. We've seen a lot of people come and go for different reasons, but the four of us have always been there from the beginning. A lot like you and Dylan, I'd assume."

Shell lowered her head, closing her eyes. "No, you know, the truth is that I've only known Dylan for a few days now."

"Seriously? It doesn't seem that way. How did you two get hooked up?"

Shell went on to tell Keon everything that had happened in the last few days. How the boy had shown up at her house first, stealing from her vegetable garden. Then about how the bandits had come and taken over her home, and then Dylan coming in and wiping them out.

"Damn," Keon said after a pause to digest it all. "I'm sorry to hear that."

Shell bowed her head again. "So am I."

Keon then turned to face her. "I just have one question. How long were you living in that town by yourself?"

The question took Shell aback. She'd thought Keon might ask something more specifically about the bandit attack or Dylan.

"A long time," Shell said.

"So why did you leave if Dylan killed all those guys?"

"Because he said they were part of a much larger group. He'd seen them during his travels and been following that convoy that ended up at my house. He said they were too big a group for us to take down on our own, and he advised me to leave."

"I see."

"I really don't know what I'm going to do now. That home was all that I knew. On top of that, I've got a responsibility to the boy now."

Keon reached over and put his hand on top of Shell's. She looked at it, then up at him. There was a kindness in his eyes, but it was all too sudden for her.

Shell jerked her hand away and stood.

"I'm sorry," Keon said.

"It's okay. Listen, I need to get some sleep."

Keon tried to stop her, but Shell left the room and headed up the stairs. He didn't follow her.

26

As Paul sat in a chair across the room, putting on his shoes and getting ready for the day, he peeked over at his sleeping wife and smiled. He picked his bag up off the floor and set it in the chair, going through it to make sure he had everything he'd need for the trip that morning.

As he zipped the bag closed, he heard the sheets stir behind him. Looking over his shoulder and seeing Brooke yawn as she stretched, Paul went to his wife's side of the bed and sat down. He stroked her hair.

"Good morning."

"Hey," she said, almost too softly for him to hear.

"How'd you sleep?"

She only shook her head, letting out another yawn.

"The little one giving you more trouble?" Paul ran his hand over her stomach.

Brooke looked down at her pregnant belly. "It wasn't that."

"What is it then? Did you have a bad dream or something?"

Grabbing Paul's hand, Brooke looked up at him. Her eyes sparkled like diamonds as she fought back tears.

"Baby, what's the matter?" Paul asked, running his hand down her cheek.

She looked to the wall to avert his gaze.

"You have to tell me," Paul said.

"Why? It's not like you're going to listen to me."

"What do you mean?"

"I have one of those feelings running through me again." Brooke looked past him at his bag, which still sat in the chair. "Like you shouldn't be going out there. It feels like something bad is going to happen."

Paul exhaled and looked away from his wife.

"See? You're doing it again, the way you react."

"It's not that, Brooke."

"What is it then?"

"I can't just bail out on going on these supply runs. As the leader of this group, it's my duty."

"And what about your duty to me? To your unborn child?"

Paul stood up and looked down at his wife. "Did you really just say that?"

"What if something happens to you out there? Do you ever think about that?"

"Everything I do and every decision I make is about you and our child. *Every* decision. When I go on these runs, all I think about is the two of you. It's why I do it."

Brooke was crying full-on now. "I want you to be here for us."

Paul sat down on the bed again and took his wife's hand. "Sweetie, I'm not going anywhere. I've told you that before. Keon and I trust each other with our lives. Nothing is going to happen while we're out there."

"You can't guarantee that."

"I can't guarantee anything. But I can tell you that I'm going to be around to see my child grow old, so help me God. You better believe that's the truth."

There was a knock on the door. It was cracked and opened slightly. Keon stood in the hallway.

"Shit, I'm sorry," Keon said.

"It's all good," Paul said. "I'll be out in just a minute."

"I was hoping I could talk to both of you, actually."

Paul looked at Brooke, then back at the door. "Now's not really a good—"

"Come on in," Brooke said.

Paul scratched his head. "Yeah, come in."

Keon walked into the room and stood against the wall across from the bed. "Sorry to interrupt you guys like this."

"It's okay, really," Brooke said. "What's going on?"

Keon took a deep breath. "I wanna talk a little bit about our visitors."

"What about 'em?" Paul asked.

"They didn't tell us their whole story."

Paul raised an eyebrow. "What do you mean?"

"Well, for starters, none of them hardly know each other."

"How do you know this?" Brooke asked.

"Because I talked to Shell last night. Well, early this morning, really. Apparently, she has some of the same problems sleeping that I do."

"Okay, so, she and Dylan don't know each other well. What else did she say?" Paul asked.

"She was living about fifty miles north of here. Some small town called Yazoo City. Sounds like she had a pretty good set-up there. A whole town to herself."

"What happened?" Brooke asked.

"Some bandits came through and took it over. That's how she met Dylan. Apparently, he showed up and killed most of them. A couple got away, but he took down several men by himself."

"Jesus," Brooke said.

Paul could tell from Keon's face and the tone in his voice that there was something more to his story.

"Why are you telling us all this?"

Keon licked his lips, then smiled. "Because I think I have an idea that might save us all."

27

Shell approached Dylan's room. She pushed the door open, remaining outside for a moment when she heard heavy breathing. She peeked inside.

Dylan lay on the ground, performing a series of bicycle crunches. He only wore his pants and boots, exposing the scars on his chest and stomach. Sweat had already collected on his chest. Shell's eyes went to the stub that had once been his arm.

At the end of his set, he lay flat on the ground with his hand on his stomach. He'd closed his eyes.

"Don't you know how to knock?" he asked without ever looking back to make eye contact with her.

"Sorry. I'll come back later."

Dylan sat up. He ran his hand through his hair before making it to his feet.

"Don't bother leaving. I'm finished, anyway."

Shell walked all the way into the room and shut the door behind her. Dylan kept his back turned to her as he shuffled through his things on the bed. The glistening sweat highlighted the dozen cuts on his back. He put on his shirt and turned around, and Shell cleared her throat. His shirt was open, and her eyes fell on his toned stomach, where he had more cuts and scars. Then she looked up into his sharp blue eyes as he buttoned the shirt.

"What did you want to talk about?"

Shell's eyes fell to Dylan's injured leg. "I'm curious how you're feeling."

"Better."

"Better as in you'll be ready to go soon?"

Dylan raised his eyebrows. "You getting anxious for me to leave all of a sudden?"

"You were exercising pretty vigorously this morning. You just look like you're about ready to go."

"Being hurt is no excuse to ignore keeping in shape."

Shell sighed. "I wanted to talk about the boy and I possibly leaving with you when you're ready to go."

"And where is this sudden change of heart coming from."

Shell crossed her arms over her chest and didn't respond.

"There's something else," Dylan said.

"There's not," Shell said. "I just think it's best if—"

Paul poked his head in the door. His eyes got big and he waved his hand in apology.

"Shit, sorry. Uh, I'll come back."

Shell looked over at Dylan, who was buttoning the last two buttons on his shirt. She then looked back to the door, where Paul had disappeared.

He thought we were...

Shell shook her head. "No, wait."

Paul opened the door again and looked into the room. "I wasn't trying to interrupt anything."

"Oh, no, no," Shell said. "I just got here. He was exercising, and... no, nothing like that."

"Just tell us why you're here," Dylan said.

Paul opened the door the rest of the way, and Keon stood beside him. He smiled as he looked in at Shell.

"I was hoping we could chat a little more about what you and I talked about at the bar," Keon said to Shell.

Dylan looked at Shell. "What conversation?"

Shell glared at Keon. "The one we had which apparently wasn't private."

She sighed and gestured for Keon and Paul to come in the room. They entered, and Keon shut the door behind him.

"I couldn't sleep last night," Shell said to Dylan. "I went downstairs and I ran into Keon. We talked, and I told him about my house and how you and I met."

"I see," Dylan said.

"I saw a packed bag in the hall," Keon said, looking at Shell. "That yours?"

Dylan narrowed his eyes at Shell. "You already packed a bag and assumed I'd take you with me?"

Shell nodded, then looked at Keon and Paul. "It's for the best. You guys have plenty to worry about without us. Lots of mouths to feed. A baby coming."

"You're right," Paul said. "And that's exactly why we came to talk to you."

Shell moved her hair behind her ear. "Okay. What do you mean?"

"I told Paul about Yazoo City," Keon said.

"Keon said you lived there for years by yourself with no trouble," Paul said. "That true?"

"It is. But it doesn't matter now. Did he tell you the part about how it was overtaken by bandits?"

"You don't know that for sure," Keon said.

"They were part of a much bigger group," Dylan said. "I saw them with my own eyes."

"But you didn't see the guys that got away return to her house with the others?" Paul asked.

Dylan snorted a laugh. "I think it's pretty safe to assume they're there now. Those assholes who got away knew it was worth coming back. Not only did they have Shell's house to come back to, but a whole fucking town for themselves."

"But that's *your* home," Keon said to Shell.

Shell shrugged and shook her head. "Not anymore, it's not."

"What if we could help you get it back?" Paul asked.

Dylan laughed, harder this time.

"Hey, what the hell is your problem, man?" Keon asked.

"You guys just don't get it. That group is full of strong, armed *men*. I bet they have half of that town on lockdown and barricaded by now."

"How many men are you talking about?" Paul asked.

"A couple of dozen, at least. Maybe more."

Paul and Keon shared a look. Then Paul looked at Shell.

"This place really as good as you described it to Keon?"

"Yeah, of course. It's called Yazoo City, but the 'City' part is deceiving. It's a really small town, but there's plenty of nice houses left over. And I had a lot of supplies at my house. I also had goats and chickens."

"Seriously?" Paul asked.

"Damn, dude, I could go for some milk and eggs," Keon said.

"Well, y'all go right on ahead," Dylan said. "You're both fools and going to get yourselves killed if you try."

"Have you guys thought of a plan?" Shell asked.

Dylan put his hand on his hip and glared at her. "Are you serious? You can't be."

"I'm just asking a simple question." She turned her attention to Paul and Keon and waited for an answer.

"We hadn't gotten that far yet," Keon said.

"We were hoping to get a little info first," Paul said. "Find out how many were in this gang, and maybe get an idea of what the area around your place is like."

"I'm going to need some time to think about all this," Shell said.

"I already know my answer," Dylan said. "You're nuts for wanting to try this."

On his way out the door, Dylan bumped shoulders with Paul. Looking down to the ground, Paul bit his lip. He took a deep breath and looked back up at Shell.

"Sorry about him," Shell said.

"Hey, you just met him. It doesn't sound like you know a whole lot about him, either."

"That's an understatement."

Keon stepped forward, moving only a couple of feet away from Shell. "Look, it's cool if you want to think about it some. But, regardless, we'd like to talk with you soon to get a little more information about where exactly your house is, what's around it and all that."

"Are you guys going even if I say no?"

"More than likely," Paul said. "We still gotta talk about it with some of the others, but more than likely, we'd go up there to at least check it out."

"We're tired of running," Keon said. "We'd obviously love for you to come with us, but we understand if you're trying to put that place behind you."

Shell sniffed and wiped sweat from her brow. She put her hands on her hips and nodded.

"The two of us are about to head out on a run," Paul said. "Think about what you want to do, all right? We can talk when we get back."

Paul turned around and left the room. But when Shell looked up, Keon was still there.

"I hope you decide to come with us." Keon shook his head. "There's nothing for you if you go east with him."

Frowning, Keon turned and exited the room. He shut the door behind him.

Shell sat on Dylan's bed. She put her elbows on her knees and leaned into her hands, exhaling into her palms.

What am I going to do?

28

THE DAY SHOWED an overcast sky which hinted at rain. It made the air more humid than it had been in recent days. Paul wiped the sweat from his brow as he and Keon approached another building. They had come on their own that morning, leaving the other scavengers behind to look after the camp. Paul didn't want to be slowed down by a larger group, as he and Keon could get in and out of buildings quickly. He also wanted to be able to discuss certain things with Keon without the others around.

Keon parked his empty shopping cart in front of the dilapidated storefront. Like with most other places, its windows had long ago been shattered, and there was nothing left but a frame where a door had once been.

"How are you feeling about us finding anything good today?" Keon asked.

Paul shook his head. "Not sure, but we've gotta try. Let's head in."

Paul gripped the handle of his machete as they entered the building, ready to unsheathe it at any moment. Keon kept his crossbow in a firing position, his finger positioned near the trigger. They circled the interior of the building, checking behind each door.

"Clear," Keon said.

"All right. Let's have a quick look around," Paul said, having little confidence they were going to find anything worth a damn.

Shelving and other wooden debris lay scattered throughout the building. Paul kneeled down to check a few boxes, but they were empty. He pushed aside debris, looking to see if anything lay underneath.

This is already looking like a bust.

Paul jerked to his right and pulled the machete halfway out of its sheath as he heard something move on the far side of the room. Keon reacted, as well, raising his crossbow and aiming it in the same direction.

A giant rat scurried across the floor, ducking through a hole in the back wall. The thing was large enough to where it could almost have been confused with a small cat or a possum. Paul sighed.

"Thank God we aren't at the point where we're hunting those to eat," Keon said.

Paul huffed out a laugh. "Yeah, we'll all be dead at that point. At least I hope so. Who the hell knows what kinds of diseases those bastards are carrying?" He eased up on his machete. "Let's keep looking around."

They continued searching the place. It had once been some kind of general store, and anything worth anything was long gone. He exhaled and kicked a shelf.

"This is a waste of time."

Keon said, "What do you mean? How is this a waste of time?"

"We're never going to find anything worth a damn."

"Not with that attitude."

"I'm serious, Keon. I mean, what are we really expecting to find in any of these buildings? You don't think everything has been picked apart by others before us in the past thirty years? This is a joke."

"Funny, 'cause this is the first I'm hearing any of this from you, and we've been doing this for a long time."

"And how much longer are we going to do it?"

"What's your point, man?"

Paul leaned against the wall. He wiped more sweat from his brow and stared outside.

"You really think Shell had a place like she says she did?"

Keon shrugged. "I don't see any reason why she would lie about it. I don't think one bit of her story now is a sham."

"I just don't understand how you would leave that and come out into a world like this. I don't care how many people were trying to take it from me. I'd fight until the end."

"Maybe that Dylan cares a little more about living than you do."

"That's hard to believe. That dude is about as lifeless as they come."

"Yeah, quite the opposite of Shell."

Paul looked over at Keon. He was staring off outside, his eyes glowing. Paul grinned.

"Whoa, hold on a second. You like that girl, don't you?"

"What?" Keon scoffed. "Get the hell out of here. No."

Paul's smile grew. "Oh, come on. You lit up like a Christmas tree just saying her name."

"Fuck. You." Keon laughed and stared at the ground. "All right, so maybe a little."

"See, I knew it, man. That's why you want her to stay."

"Now, that part's not true. I want her to stay for a hell of a lot more reasons than that. I want her and that boy to stay so they can survive. You and I both know that the best way to keep on is in packs."

"Well, maybe she'll come around and make the right decision."

Keon turned to Paul. "We're going to check the place out regardless, though, aren't we?"

Paul bit his lip as he looked at his friend. Then snarls came from outside, shifting his attention out there. He renewed the hold on his machete and Keon raised his crossbow.

Outside, demons walked into view from either side of the front of the store. Three appeared from the right, and another two from the left. They looked into the building, making eye contact with Paul and Keon.

"Get ready for some company," Keon said.

"Let them come in here to us, and try to save your ammo. Watch my back."

Paul pulled out his machete and approached the front. The first Demon came through the door, reaching out to him. He raised the machete and drove the blade down into the creature's head. It fell limply to the ground and Paul pulled back on the machete, easily able to dislodge it from its skull.

Two more creatures poured through the door. Paul kicked the first one backward, sending it flying back through the entryway. Then he swung the machete at the other. He didn't have the time to aim his blow, and grazed the Demon's ear, cutting it off and burying the machete's blade into the thing's shoulder. He kicked it against the wall, his machete pulling out with a wet slurp. The Demon had slammed against the wall, and Keon pulled his trigger and sent a bolt into the Demon's forehead.

Paul refocused on the outside and saw that a few more Demons had shown up.

"This isn't working," Keon said. "If they fill this place, we're screwed."

Paul backed up, keeping his focus on the Demons coming for the open storefront. "I think I saw a way out through the back. Let's go."

Keon fired one more bolt, hitting a Demon in the shoulder and knocking it back. Then he turned around and led Paul through the back. They came into what had likely once been a storage room. As Paul had seen, there was a door at the back of the room, and sun drifted in beneath it.

Paul jumped in front of Keon. "Let's get the hell out of here."

"Paul, wait!" Keon yelled.

But Paul had already pushed through the unlocked door. He was greeted by a Demon lunging in from his right. His eyes went wide as the creature came at him, its arms outstretched and mouth open.

The Demon grabbed onto Paul's shoulders. It snapped at him, but Paul managed to just hold the creature at bay. Its momentum sent them down onto the ground.

When Paul's back slammed against the concrete, he cried out and his right hand came loose from holding the Demon's torn shirt. The Demon snapped its jaws at Paul's shoulder and missed.

The Demon's weight was suddenly off of Paul as Keon kicked it in the stomach and pushed it off of his friend. He then stood over the creature and fired his crossbow, point blank at its skull. The Demon let out one snarling scream before the bolt entered through its forehead.

Paul gasped for air. He looked at his arms and hands,

searching for bites. There were none. Keon reached down and offered his hand, pulling Paul up.

Patting down his shirt and pants, Paul checked himself once more for bites. Then he laughed.

"What the fuck is so funny?" Keon asked.

"Brooke was worried about me going on this run because she had a bad feeling something was going to happen to me. But I told her I'd be fine. Looks like I won."

Keon shook his head. "You're an asshole, you know that?"

"Maybe, but you love me."

"No, I tolerate your white ass because for some reason I feel like I need you."

Snarling came from the front of the building and around the side. The other Demons were looking for them.

"Let's get the hell out of here," Keon said.

29

In one of the vacant second story rooms, Shell had come across a children's book called *Brer Rabbit in the Briar Patch*. The charming and colorful blue cover depicted a grinning rabbit skipping down a dirt path, and when she showed it to the boy, his eyes lit up. This alone brought a smile to her face. So, they found a place with enough light for her to read it to him.

She sat against the wall under the window, the light shining straight down onto the pages. Shell held the book with one hand and wrapped her other arm around the boy, who nestled into her chest.

She was on the last couple of pages of the book when she looked up and saw Dylan leaning against the door frame. They shared a brief gaze before Shell looked back down to the book and continued reading the story.

"The End," she said as she got to the last page and closed the book. She nestled the boy's hair. "What did you think of that?"

With glowing eyes, the young kid smiled and nodded at Shell. She pulled him in closer, giving him a tight side hug.

"Where'd you learn to read?" Dylan asked.

"My friend, Lewis."

"He the same one who taught you to shoot?"

Shell nodded. "He's the one who taught me everything."

There was an awkward moment of silence before Shell asked, "Did you want to talk to me about something?"

"Maybe it should just be the two of us."

Glancing down at the boy, Shell said, "There's nothing you can say to me right now that he shouldn't hear." She glanced at the boy, and he nodded and stayed put.

Dylan shrugged then stepped into the room. "You're not seriously thinking about going back up to your town with these people, are you?"

"I'm not sure."

"You're making a huge mistake even considering it."

Shell narrowed her eyes. "Why do you care so much?"

Dylan stared at her with his now infamous cold glare. He didn't say anything in response to her question.

"I'm serious. You didn't want the two of us joining you in the first place. I had to practically beg you to let us come along. You won't tell me a damn thing about where you're headed, but it doesn't seem anything is going to stop you from going. Why the hell should I follow you blindly to somewhere others are telling you not to go?"

"They don't know what they're talking about."

"Yeah?" Shell stood up. "And how do you know that?"

Again, Dylan gave her the silent treatment, responding only with a malevolent stare.

"That's what I thought," Shell said.

"Frankly, I don't give a damn if you follow me or not. It's not like that was ever the plan. I'll be just fine on my own. Not sure I can say the same about you two."

"I did quite all right fending for myself before you came

along. Besides, maybe me being with this group will keep me alive longer."

Dylan shook his head. "Not if this group plans to go and try to take your town back."

Shell's nostrils flared. She formed a fist, clutching at her perspiring palms. A look at the boy briefly calmed her. She could see in his expression that he was scared, and she didn't want to further that. She took a deep breath, ready to refute Dylan, when she heard a commotion outside. A horse neighed, and people spoke loudly. Shell looked out the window. Then she turned to Dylan, who was looking out the door and down the hall, toward the front of the building.

"Come on," Dylan said. "Stay close to me."

Shell took the boy's hand without hesitating and followed Dylan out the door. They moved down the hallway, staying close to the wall. When he arrived at the corner, Dylan had a view to the lobby and stopped. He looked around the corner. Then he turned to Shell and gestured for her to join him.

Standing beside Dylan, Shell glanced out towards the front of the building, about twenty yards from where they were. A group of around a dozen people, all on horseback, had arrived at the hotel.

"We know there's someone in there," one of the men said. "We heard y'all. Now come on out, and it'll make it easy on all of us."

"Should we go out there?" Shell asked.

"No," Dylan said sternly. "We're staying right here."

"I'm counting to three," the man said. "If someone doesn't answer my call by then, then I can assure you things aren't going to be pretty."

Shell wanted to go out there. Dylan could apparently sense her feelings, because he shook his head.

"One," the man said. "Two."

Three people appeared in the lobby and approached the door.

"Oh, no," Shell said.

It was Brooke, Katrina, and Caleb. Brooke led the group, her hands raised to show she wasn't armed. Neither Katrina nor Caleb had their hands up. Shell only hoped they hadn't all decided to walk outside unarmed.

"We can't let them walk out there alone," Shell said. "We've got to—"

"We'll stay here," Dylan said, cutting her off.

Shell exhaled, then took a deep breath. She wanted to be there for her new friends, especially with Paul and Keon off on a run.

"Well, look at this, boys," the leader said to the others in his group. "We've got a pregger, a beautiful black woman, and some dude who looks like a mechanic. Sounds like the start of a bad joke."

The group behind him laughed.

"What is it that you want?" Brooke asked.

"Whoa, you want to jump into the fun already?" The leader dismounted the horse.

Shell bit her lip. "We can't just stand here and do nothing." She stepped forward, but Dylan grabbed her arm.

"Let go of me!"

Dylan yanked her around the corner and out of sight. He moved within inches of her face.

"You're not going to do a damn bit of good if you go marching out there. There's too many of them. Brooke's smart, and she's pregnant. I doubt they're going to hurt her. Let her handle them. We need to avoid a confrontation, not start a war."

Dylan let go of Shell, who breathed rapidly. He looked

around the corner again, and once Shell was calm, she rejoined him.

"For starters," the leader said to Brooke, "we're looking for some people."

Brooke shrugged. "No one's come through here, so I'm not sure we'll be too much help to you."

"That so? Well, maybe you should think about that a little harder. See, these people we're looking for are murderers."

Shaking her head, Brooke said, "I'm sorry, but I don't think we've seen—"

"There's three of them. Well, two and a half. One of 'em is a little boy. Then there's a girl, either in her late teens or early twenties. And the star of the show is some long-haired, one-armed punk ass who thinks he's some kinda fuckin' cowboy or somethin'."

Caleb said, "Like the lady here said, we ain't seen no one come through here. Especially not anyone with those descriptions. No little boy. No girl. No freak with one arm. Nothin'."

"That's interesting, isn't it, boys?" the leader said.

"Sure is, Dean" one of the others said.

Dean nodded at Brooke. "Then you wouldn't mind if we had a look around, would you? See, there's a big bounty on these three, and I'd like to collect it."

Shell jerked her head back. Dylan apparently saw the surprise in her face as he shrugged.

"Word travels fast amongst some of these gangs," he said.

Then Shell watched as Katrina stepped in between the man and Brooke. "The hell with that."

"Katrina," Brooke said, grabbing her friend's shoulder. "Don't."

"Don't what? We aren't gonna let these guys ride on in here and step all over our shit. This is our building. We found it. And just because they think we aren't telling the truth, well, that's their goddamn problem."

"Well, aren't you the little firecracker?" Dean said, smiling. "I've been known to have me a little jungle fever. I bet you're a wild animal in the sack. Maybe you and I oughta—"

Katrina punched Dean in the face before he could finish. There was a gasp amongst everyone looking on as the man's head turned to the side and he grabbed his cheek. When he looked back at Katrina, though, Dean laughed. She stood her ground, her shoulders squared.

Dean wrapped his large hand around her throat. Caleb moved forward to stop him, but the man quickly raised a knife with his free hand and held it up.

"Move any closer, and I'll jam this into her fucking skull."

Some of the other bandits drew knives and bows, aiming them at Caleb and Brooke.

Katrina gasped for air, trying to pry the man's hands from her throat.

Shell breathed rapidly. "We have to do something!"

Dylan still didn't move.

Shell could see Dean's lips moving as he said something to Katrina, but she was too far away to hear it. She wasn't so far away, though, that she couldn't see Katrina's heavy gasps.

"Please, stop it!" Brooke said to the man. "Let her go!"

Katrina's eyes closed slightly, and her hands started to go limp.

"Goddamnit, stop!" Caleb said.

Dean finally let go, dropping Katrina to the ground. He then bent over her and pointed his knife at her face.

"You touch me again, I swear to Christ I'll carve out

those chocolate eyes and make you listen to me eat them. Do you understand me?"

Katrina rolled onto her side as she held her throat. Dean kicked her in the ribs. She cried out and coughed, and the man went back to his horse.

As he mounted the animal, Dean gestured toward Caleb. "What's in that bag?"

From her vantage point, Shell now noticed that Caleb was holding the backpack they'd put all their medical supplies in. It included all that Shell had given them for helping out with Dylan's injuries, which was most of what she'd had left.

"Nothing," Caleb said.

"Bullshit," one of the men said.

One corner of Dean's mouth lifted into a smile. "Yeah, I smell bullshit, too."

"I don't care what you *think* you smell," Caleb said. "There ain't nothing in here."

Dean shook his head. "Listen, killer, you don't want me to have to get back off of this horse."

"Please," Brooke said. "That's got all our medical supplies in it. You can't—"

Dean steered his horse over to Brooke, who stepped back. He said, "I can't what?"

Brooke only stared up at him, shaking her head. Even from a distance, Shell could tell she was fighting back tears.

"Take it," Dean said to his men again.

A guy with shaggy blonde hair dismounted his horse and approached Caleb. Caleb held the strap of the bag tight in his hand and scowled as the guy reached out for it.

"Come on, asshole. Hand it over."

Caleb waited another moment before exhaling and

offering the bag to the man. The blonde bandit snatched it away. He laughed as he opened it and searched through it.

"There's some good shit in here, boss." He handed the bag to Dean.

Brooke and Caleb checked on Katrina as Dean rummaged through the bag. When he'd finished, the leader tipped his hat to Brooke.

"I must say, thank you for this. We won't let it go to waste."

Dean kicked his horse and turned to leave. He'd only gone a few feet when he pulled back on the reins and turned around to look at her again.

"Oh, and if I find out that you do in fact know those murderers," he said, raising the knife and staring at the tip, "then I'll be coming back here and you'll be having a C-section. Ain't nobody gonna be taking this bounty from me."

Dean kicked his horse again and took off, the other bandits in his group hollering as they sped away.

30

"THE OTHERS ARE gonna be disappointed that we didn't bring anything back," Keon said.

"It'll be all right," Paul answered. "There's still a little bit of that deer left to hopefully tie everyone over for another day or so."

"We might want to at least think about going back and getting that cart. Not as many of those around anymore."

"We'll make another sweep by that area tomorrow. Hopefully, the Demons will have cleared out by then."

Paul and Keon caught back up with the main road after staying low behind other buildings to escape from the horde of Demons. The King Edward towered into the sky only a couple of blocks away.

Paul said, "We should try and get out early again tomorrow so we can—"

He cut his sentence off when he heard the hooves of horses beating against the concrete, and men hollering. The sound grew louder with each passing moment.

"What the hell is that?" Keon asked.

Paul saw the first man on horseback swing around the

corner up the road. He threw his arms around Keon, tackling him to the ground behind the remains of a pickup truck.

Keon groaned. "Shit, man."

"Get on the other side of this truck. Quick!"

They crawled to the side of the truck. Paul tucked his legs in to give himself a low profile and to be more out of sight from the men racing down the road.

The road quaked as at least a dozen horses scampered down it. The men in the group sounded like a gang from an old Western film, hootin' and hollerin' as they raced by. The horses slowed to a walk only a couple of dozen yards away from where Paul and Keon were hiding.

"No one fucks with us," one of the men said.

Another said, "You should have choked that bitch out, boss."

"Did you see the look on that pregnant one?" asked another.

Paul's eyes went wide. His heart dropped.

Brooke.

He started to stand, but Keon grabbed his arm. He pulled Paul back down.

"Hold up, man. I hear them, but you gotta wait until they're gone."

Paul bit his lip. He was torn between wanting to run back to his wife and wanting to chase after those bastards and rip every one of their hearts out.

The horses sprinted again, and soon, the hollers and horses faded. Keon glanced around the back of the truck.

"They're gone."

It only took those two words for Paul to jump to his feet and take off towards the King Edward. Keon ran behind him without protest.

When they arrived at the hotel, most of the almost twenty people who made up the group had collected outside, and more were coming out. They stood in a semi-circle, all looking down at the ground. Caleb glanced up to see Paul and Keon running towards them and others looked their way. Caleb walked to meet them.

"What the hell happened?" Paul asked.

"Everything's all right," Caleb said.

Paul slowed down and tried looking between the people to see what they were looking at. His heart raced.

"Where the hell is Brooke?"

"She's fine," Caleb said.

"Paul?" Brooke said from the center of the crowd.

Paul hurried through, pushing people out of the way.

Brooke was sitting next to Katrina, who lay flat on the ground. Both of them were crying, and Katrina had her hand on her neck as she breathed heavily.

"Oh, shit," Keon said. He rushed to his sister's side.

"She's okay, Keon," Brooke said.

"What in the fuck happened?" Keon ran his hand over his sister's forehead. "Trina, Jesus Christ."

"Give her a little room to breathe," Brooke said. She turned around. "All of you."

"Come on," Paul said to the others, directing them to back off.

"Will someone tell me what the hell happened?" Keon asked.

"Some men showed up here," Brooke said.

"All those guys on horses?" Paul asked.

Brooke nodded. "They had weapons and numbers. They demanded we come out to talk or they were going to hurt us." Brooke was crying harder now. Paul went to her, kneeling and wrapping his arm around her.

"They were looking for three 'murderers,'" Caleb said. "A child, a woman, and a scruffy drifter."

"I told them we hadn't seen them and didn't know who they were talking about," Brooke said. "But the guy didn't believe us. He threatened me. Katrina stepped in. She hit the guy and he nearly choked the life out of her."

"Son of a bitch," Keon said. "I'm gonna fucking kill him."

Paul felt similarly. He clenched his jaw, furious. What kind of man threatened a pregnant woman and choked another?

Keon drew his machete from his waist and turned the direction the men had run off. His shoulders moved up and down from his heavy breathing, and he took several steps away from the west of the group.

"What the hell are you doing?" Caleb asked.

"What the hell do you think? I'm gonna go after those motherfuckers."

"Calm down, Keon," Paul said.

"Don't tell me to fucking calm down! That piece of shit put his hands on my sister's throat, and now I'm gonna rip his out!"

"Look, I'm pissed, too. He threatened my pregnant wife, for Christ's sake." Paul felt a migraine coming on and his body fumed with anger.

"Who were those guys?" asked Amy, a sixty-year-old woman and one of the older members of the group.

"They were looking for us."

Everyone turned and followed the female voice to the entrance of the hotel. Shell, Dylan, and the boy had stepped out through the front doorway and stood side by side.

Paul stood. "We saw them when we were on our way back. Were they part of that group that took over Shell's town?"

Dylan shook his head. "There's a bounty out on us now. That gang must've made it back to Shell's and seen what I did to their men."

"Shit," Paul said.

"The gang waiting back in that town is easily triple that size."

"What the hell are we supposed to do, man?" Keon asked, standing. "They almost killed my sister, and they took off with all our food and supplies."

"You'll cut your losses. Be thankful that your sister is alive, and find more food."

"No, see, I don't think it's that easy," Paul said, stepping forward. "We aren't just going to let some raiders come through here and threaten our people and take off with all our shit."

"Be glad that all they did was threaten them."

"You kidding me?" Keon pointed at his injured sister. "Look at what they did to her."

"She's breathing. Be thankful."

"No, fuck that, man." Keon moved towards Dylan, but Paul held him back.

As he held his friend back, Paul stared down Dylan. He shook his head.

"You're nothing but a coward. That's all."

"Call me what you will," Dylan said, stepping forward. "But I'll be breathing by the time all this is done, because I plan on getting as far away from this mess as possible."

Paul laughed and shook his head. "If that's how you wanna live, then fine. But I'm not going to let those assholes get away with this. If you could take down a small group of them by yourself, then I'm sure we'll do fine against the rest of them." Paul looked past Dylan at Shell. "I wanna know where your town is. Let's go talk so you can give me directions."

Shell stepped forward. "I don't have to give you directions." She looked at Dylan and said, "Because I'm going to take you there."

Dylan shook his head, staring back at her. "Then you're as dumb as they are."

He turned around and walked back inside the hotel.

31

When the sun woke Paul the following morning, he sat up and rubbed his eyes. He'd barely caught a wink of sleep, having tossed and turned most of the night with too much on his mind to give it a chance to rest. He got up from the bed and slipped into his pants and shirt. He'd already packed his bag the previous night. There was nothing else to do now but wait.

He sat in a chair across the room from the bed with his hands folded in his lap. He watched his wife. She lay on her side, her eyes closed as she slept peacefully. As he watched her sleep, he recalled some of his favorite memories involving her. When they'd met. The first time they'd kissed. Their wedding day, and how it had been a day of joy for everyone in the camp. A time for them, for at least one day, to forget about the fucked up world they lived in. Then he thought of the moment Brooke had told him he was going to be a father.

And he looked forward. He closed his eyes and thought about his unborn child. He pictured lying beside Brooke and holding his baby for the first time. Only, they weren't on some street corner or in some rundown hotel. They were in a beautiful house, with a warm and comfortable bed. Their friends were there, and everyone was happy. Paul could think of nothing more he wanted than to live that moment.

Paul opened his eyes and came out of the thought when he heard Brooke stir. He smiled as he saw his wife's green eyes glow in the sun and look at him.

"Hey," she said softly before she yawned.

"Good morning."

"Did you get any sleep?"

Paul shook his head. He went to the bed and lay on his side, cuddling up to his wife's backside. He wrapped his arm around Brooke, kissing her on the cheek. Then he rested his hand on her belly.

They lay in silence. Paul ran his hand over Brooke's baby bump, and they looked out the window to the bright sky.

"You need to be here when our child is born," Brooke said, breaking the silence.

"I will be. This should only take a few days. We'll be back before you know it."

Brooke took Paul's hand and gripped it tight. Her eyes turned glassy and a tear rolled down her cheek.

"What is it?" Paul asked.

"Those men were evil, Paul. I saw it in their eyes. They had no remorse for anything. If the men who took over Shell's town are anything like them…"

"Where else can we go? I'm tired of running, Brooke."

Brooke turned to look into her husband's eyes. "But what makes you so sure you can beat them?"

"What makes you ask that?"

More tears moved down Brooke's cheeks. "You didn't see these men. They were ruthless. I mean, what if Dylan is right? What if this is all just a big mistake?"

"It's not a mistake, okay? This is just what we have to do."

"But why? Can't we keep moving, away from that gang, and find somewhere else?"

"Where else?" Frustration grew in Paul's voice. "How much farther do we have to go, Brooke?"

"Don't get upset with me. I'm just scared."

Paul sighed as he kissed his wife's hand. "I'm scared, too. But I'm also tired of running. You can't have our baby here, Brooke. And you can't have it on the highway. If that town is half of what Shell described, then I can't see you having it anywhere but there. And I know this sounds crazy, but I think she was brought here for a reason. So that we could help her get her town back and we could stop running."

Brooke didn't reply. She merely held her husband's hand and let him continue to spoon her. After a few more minutes, Paul got up and grabbed his bag off the table.

"I have to go meet the others downstairs before we leave."

"All right."

Brooke was no longer crying, but her face was red from doing so. Paul went to her and leaned down to kiss her forehead and run his hand through her hair. Then he went to the door. When he got there, he stopped and turned around.

"Eloise."

"What?" Brooke asked.

"That's what we should call our daughter."

"I thought you hated that name."

Paul smiled and shook his head. "It's the most beautiful name I've ever heard."

"Well, what if it's a boy like you want?"

Paul's grin grew and he shook his head. "It's not going to

be a boy. We're going to have a little girl, and she's going to be just as gorgeous as you."

Brooke's face glowed. Her eyes welled again, and Paul himself fought back tears. He had to stay focused.

"I love you," he said. "I'll see you downstairs in a bit."

He shut the door behind him and wiped his eyes. Then he took a deep breath and headed downstairs.

32

SHELL STARED at herself in the mirror as she put her hair up. Her reflection only appeared in the top left corner, as the rest of the glass had cracked and shattered.

When she'd finished putting her hair up, she stayed in front of the mirror and stared at her face. She hardly recognized herself. The last few days had felt like years. Her life had changed so much in the previous week, and her tired eyes and hardened cheeks reflected that.

She saw a shadow in the mirror and turned around to see the boy. Kneeling in front of him, she wiped a smudge of dirt from under his eye.

"Everything's going to be okay. I promise you. They're going to take real good care of you here while I'm gone."

He didn't say anything. He only wrapped his arms around her and hugged her. Shell held him tight, fighting back the urge to cry.

Then Shell stood, throwing her backpack over her shoulder. She took the boy's hand and led him out the door. They walked downstairs to the lobby and through the front door, to where everyone waited outside at the entrance. She was the last one to arrive.

"We were beginning to wonder if you'd bailed on us," Keon said, smiling.

"Sorry to disappoint you, but here I am."

Brooke stood nearby, and Shell walked the boy over to her. She kneeled down again.

"You remember Brooke, right?"

Brooke leaned over. "Hey, sweetie."

Shell said, "Brooke's gonna let you hang out with her while we're gone. That sound good?"

The boy nodded, a small grin on his face. Brooke took his hand and Shell joined the others.

"This everyone?" Shell asked, glancing around at the group of nearly twenty.

Paul nodded. "Only two people are staying behind, along with Brooke and the four kids."

"And we've already rationed out the food we had left and given most to them. I figure we'll be able to find some more food for us along the way."

"Good idea."

"Speaking of good ideas," Katrina said, looking at Shell. "Are you sure it's the best idea for us to follow the train tracks?"

"I do. The train tracks lead right into Yazoo City and are only about a mile from my house. And from what you all have said, the highways aren't exactly the best way to travel if we're trying to avoid more bandits."

"What about Demons?" Katrina asked.

"Demons are going to be a threat no matter which way we go," Keon said.

"Yeah, but walking through the woods and the fields, away from the roads?" Katrina shook her head.

"We'll deal with them as they come," Paul said. "Like Keon said, we can't avoid the Demons no matter where we go." He looked at Shell. "But if this place is half of what you say it is, then it'll be worth it."

Shell smiled at him, and as she was looking his way, she saw Dylan standing against a wall by himself about twenty feet away.

"Let's go ahead and get going," Paul said. "We want to make as much progress as we can today."

Everyone started to scatter.

"I'll catch up with you guys," Shell said.

Paul and Keon both looked over to Dylan, then nodded at Shell.

"Take your time," Paul said.

Shell adjusted her backpack, slipping it all the way onto both her shoulders. She held the straps with her thumbs as she walked up to Dylan.

"You sure you don't want to join us?"

"You sure you don't wanna stay alive?"

Shell rolled her eyes. "Nothing you can say is going to make me change my mind."

"I know."

"So you ready to tell me where you're going and why?"

"Doesn't matter. It's a personal journey. Always was. I see that more now than I did before."

"It's always going to be a personal journey if you're never going to be willing to let others become close to you."

"I lost faith in people a long time ago," Dylan said.

Shell looked away, biting her lip in frustration. There was so much she wanted to say. She wanted to curse him. She wanted to hit him. But in the end, she knew none of that would be worth it.

"That said, maybe there's a chance in that changing," Dylan said. "Maybe you brought me back a little bit."

Shell jerked her head back as she looked up at the drifter. "Did you just say something nice?"

Dylan stepped away from the wall. "You take care of yourself, and the boy." He extended his hand for Shell to shake.

Shell glanced at it and then up at Dylan. She pushed his hand away and leaned into his chest, and wrapped her arms around him.

After a moment, Dylan's hand landed on her back. She pulled away a few seconds later, her hands on his shoulders.

"I hope you find whatever it is you're looking for."

She faced around and walked to catch up to the others.

Don't turn around.

She told herself this over and over again, but she couldn't resist.

She turned around.

But when she did, no one was there.

As mysteriously as he'd appeared, Dylan had vanished.

Paul turned to his wife when they reached the train tracks. He'd already been holding onto one of her hands, and now he took her other. Her eyes filled with tears and he ran his thumb across her cheek to wipe them away as they fell.

"There's no reason to cry. We aren't saying goodbye."

"I know, but I'm scared."

"So am I, but that's just more motivation for me to make it back here to meet our little girl."

Brooke laughed, and the tears came out now. Paul hugged her, running his hands up and down her back. As he was holding her, he saw Ronald, one of the men coming on the journey with them, hugging his wife and his little boy. Then he watched Shell approach the group alone. He'd held out hope that Dylan would change his mind. As much as he hated the bastard, Paul knew they'd have a better shot against the gang if he were with them. Shell looked Paul's way for a second, before heading over to join the others. Paul pulled away from his wife.

"You going to be all right?"

Brooke nodded. "Amy is here in case something happens. She can help me deliver the baby."

"Eloise."

Brooke laughed, still crying. She wiped her eyes and said, "Eloise."

Paul kissed his wife. He ran his hand down her cheek, and it felt like the first time they'd kissed. And he knew it wouldn't be the last, even as scared as both of them were.

"I love you," he said.

"I love you, too."

He took a deep breath, and then turned around. He walked over and joined the rest of the group.

"You ready for this?" Keon asked, clearly able to tell his friend was hurting.

"I'm good. Let's get going."

Everyone said their goodbyes to those staying, and finally they started down the tracks.

Don't turn around, Paul. Keep looking forward.

But he couldn't help it. Paul had to turn around and look at his wife.

She was no longer crying. A smile stretched across her face, and she blew a kiss at her husband. Paul returned the gesture and mouthed the words, "I love you."

When he turned forward again, he didn't look back until

they'd rounded a corner and those they'd left behind were
out of sight.

I hope I'm making the right decision.

33

SHELL WALKED ALONE, the anchor of the group. She looked out into the open countryside, taking in the beautiful scenery. When she wasn't surrounded by the vacant, ruined city, it became easier to wonder what the world had once been like. The world before her. She'd only heard the stories from Lewis and the others who'd lived in the town with her, and who had lived over thirty years ago before everything had changed.

She turned her attention forward and saw Keon sneaking a look back at her. He walked near the middle of the pack alongside his sister. Shell smiled when he looked at her, and he returned the expression. He said something to his sister, then stepped out of line and waited for the group in front of Shell to pass.

"You're going to leave your sister alone like that?" Shell smiled again.

"Believe me, she probably fist-pumped when I walked away. I annoy her enough."

Shell laughed.

"Besides, you look like you could use some company back here. Trina can find someone else to talk to."

"How do you know I don't want to walk alone?"

Keon raised his hands up. "Cool. That's all good. I just wanted to—"

"I'm kidding." Shell laughed again. "You can walk with me."

"Oh, okay," Keon said, relieved. He moved in next to Shell, falling back into line.

Keon didn't say anything after that, and Shell could feel a strange tension.

"I thought you came back here to talk to me," Shell said to break the silence.

"Well, to give you some company, more or less."

"Either is fine."

"You could tell me more about your town," Keon said.

"Not much to say. It's just a little town. Nothing like Jackson. But I will say that Yazoo is in much better shape. There's a lot of great houses for everyone to live in. My house is gorgeous, though probably not as much as it once was. But I was happy there."

"And you're going to be happy there again."

Shell glanced up at him and smiled. "I hope you're right."

There was another awkward silence. Shell could tell Keon was trying to work up the guts to say something.

"Did you really lose track of how long you were there alone? I'm sorry if asking that is rude. I just couldn't imagine being stuck somewhere by myself for a long time. I feel like I'd go—"

"Five years, three months, and eleven days."

Keon stared at her, his jaw slack. He was silent for

several moments. Shell kept her focus forward until she finally looked over at him again.

"Um, wow," he said. "But you said earlier that you weren't sure. How do you—"

"A week or so after the last person died, I started keeping track of the days." Shell shrugged. "Something about it just felt necessary."

"Jesus Christ, Shell. That's a long damn time. I don't think I would have lasted that long without cracking. How did you do it?"

Shell pictured Lewis' face. She thought of the conversations they'd had, and what he'd told her in the moments before he'd passed on. "*You have to live,*" he'd said.

"I made a promise to someone."

Keon shook his head. "You've got to be the strongest person I've ever met."

"I don't know about that."

"No, I'm serious. I'm just happy you're on my side."

"Yeah, well, I don't know what would have happened if you guys wouldn't have shown up when you did. Those Deads were overwhelming us."

"You would have gotten out of it. I've seen you shoot, remember?"

Shell laughed.

Keon said, "Everything happens for a reason."

"Do you really believe that?"

Keon nodded. "I do. I think that we all ended up there at the same time so that we could be here now, doing this. On our way back to your town. You wouldn't have gone back to it without us, and we'd still be on the road, trying to find somewhere we could call home again."

"We don't have my house back yet."

"But we will."

Shell pursed her lips. "How can you be so sure?"

"Because I know we won't lose.."

"Well, we *could* lose."

Keon looked to the front of the group. He shook his head as he pointed to Paul.

"That's not an option for him. Trust me. He's going to do everything in his power to make sure he gets home to his wife and that he sees his child be born."

These men will have wills of their own.

Shell hesitated to share her thoughts out loud. She wanted to believe they would easily be able to walk into her town and take it back. But with the way Dylan had spoken of the gang awaiting them, she couldn't be sure. She was scared.

34

STANDING at the front of the group by himself, Paul looked to the sky. Though he didn't know exactly how long it'd been since they'd left, they had been walking for hours. The sun hung low in the horizon with night fast approaching. He didn't travel when it got dark, not when he could help it. Not only did the darkness make it more dangerous to traverse the landscape, but the group was more vulnerable if they were tired. And Paul's feet and calves had begun to ache, so he could only think the others were wearing thin as well.

Katrina and Caleb moved up to the front to join him.

"What are you thinking?" Katrina asked Paul. "It'll be dark soon."

"I'd like to try to find somewhere with some shelter. If we can help it, I'd like to be out of sight of any Demons or raiders. It looks like it could rain, too."

"There's nothing out in front of us," Caleb said. "It could be another hour before we come across something."

Paul looked ahead. His friend was right. In front of them, he saw nothing but train tracks surrounded by trees and, beyond those, open plains filled with nothing. He pointed to a bend in the tracks some half-a-mile ahead.

"We'll head around that corner there, and if we don't find a building or something at that point, we'll make camp outside."

"Maybe there'll be an empty train car or something," Caleb said.

"We'll keep going and see what we find," Paul said. "Fall back and let the others know."

Paul drowned out the sound of Katrina and Caleb telling the others his plan. He thought of his wife. He hadn't even been away from her a day yet, but leaving her had already taken its toll on him. Paul had been used to spending hours away from her while he went on supply runs and hunting. And while those situations were dangerous, he had never done anything like this. He felt confident she and the others who'd been left behind would be safe, but what if more bandits came through the city and found them when he was more than a few blocks away?

You can't let those thoughts creep into your head, Paul. You will make it home to your wife, no matter what.

He refocused on the walk, keeping his eyes peeled for any threats that could emerge around them. When they came to the bend in the tracks, Paul said a prayer to himself, hoping they'd find shelter on the other side.

But as they headed forward, Paul saw nothing. He shifted to try and get a better look, hoping that the straight-away would come into sight and there would be some building for them to find refuge in for the night.

He heard a familiar noise then and clenched his fist. His nostrils flared.

Paul saw the large group of Demons before they saw his group, and they were gathered around something. They stood in front of a building, just off the side of the tracks. Paul ducked down, moving off of the rails as he motioned to those behind him. He used hand gestures to tell the others to get down, and he slid down onto the hill on the side of the tracks. Breathing heavily, Paul looked over at Keon.

"I don't think they saw us," Keon said.

Paul crawled up the short hill and looked over the railroad tracks at the group of Demons. There were at least a dozen of them, but it was hard to tell for sure. They'd gathered in a circle, and the ones in the back of the pack were trying to shove their way through to get at whatever had garnered their attention. Paul saw between the cracks that they were burying their teeth into some large animal, likely a deer.

On the other side of the deer was a building. The vinyl siding showed its age with several holes and cracks in it. But the roof appeared to be intact, and the place looked large enough to house their whole group for an evening.

Paul slid back down the slope and lay on his back.

"That building they're blocking seems perfect for us," he said. "We've got to clear them out so we can make camp there for the night."

"How many of them are there?" Katrina asked.

"At least a dozen. It looks like they found them some dinner—a deer or something."

"Then let's get those bastards while they're distracted," Ronald said.

"Just because they don't know we're here and they're gathered up doesn't mean we can jump in there and start slaying them," Paul said.

"Why not?" Ronald asked. "Seems simple enough to me."

"Man, shut up and listen to Paul," Keon said.

"Yeah, let's wait and try to come up with a strategy," Julia said.

"Fuck off," Ronald said to both Keon and Julia.

Julia tried to hop over Katrina to get at Ronald, but Katrina grabbed onto her arm and held her back. Others began chiming in, raising the sound level coming from the group. Paul sweat as the noise grew louder.

"Everyone, shut up," Paul said. "We're going to—"

Out of his peripheral vision, Paul saw something come over the top of the hill. None of the others saw the Demon, and Paul couldn't react fast enough to stop it.

The monster snarled as it fell forward, losing traction on the gravel hillside. Ronald was so wrapped up in being frustrated with Julia that he didn't see the monster before it fell on top of him. The Demon's head landed on Ronald's stomach and Ronald screamed.

Paul jumped to his feet and raised his machete as he hurried over to Ronald. He yelled, "Look out!" to the others before he swung the machete downward, landing it with a blow into the Demon's back. He pulled out his machete and swung again, hitting it in the neck this time. The third strike sent the blade through the monster's skull. It let out one fading snarl, then fell limp on Ronald's body.

Ronald continued to scream. Paul looked back to see the other Demons had left their prey to follow the commotion.

"We've got to get this thing off him," Martin said. "Help me."

"Jesse, Tim, and Stewart, stay with him," Paul said. "Everyone else, come with me."

Paul charged up the hill, greeting a Demon that was about to slide down the slope. The Demon had the higher ground, so Paul drove both his palms into its stomach, sending it back and giving him more space to get onto the tracks and on level ground with the horde. The Demon had tripped backward on the tracks and fallen onto its back, so Paul turned his focus to the nearest creature. He swung his machete, hitting the Demon in the jugular and severing its head from its body.

The Demons had spread out, making it easier for the humans to focus on taking out one at a time. Blades swung through the air, and arrows and bolts soared into their targets. Within a couple of minutes, they'd taken down the horde of Demons, including a few others which had come out of the building and moved in from behind it.

It hadn't been an easy fight, but when it was finished, no more of the humans had gotten hurt.

Paul hurried back to where the others were, at the bottom of the hill on the side of the tracks.

Ronald lay on his back. Blood soaked his clothes, and Tim was pressing a shirt against his stomach. Ronald breathed slowly, his eyes bloodshot, his arms dangling at his sides.

A grim expression covered Tim's face as he looked up at Paul. He pulled the shirt back to reveal a bite wound next to Ronald's navel.

Paul sighed, looking away from the wound. He covered his face with his hands as Keon and Katrina arrived on either side of him.

"Goddamnit," Keon said.

Julia stumbled down the hill, falling at his side. Her hands quaked as she reached for his face. When she turned back to Paul, tears flooded her eyes.

"We have to move him into the building before it gets dark and before more of those things come. Anyone, come help me move him."

She moved behind him, and Ronald grunted. "No."

"We can help you," Julia said, still not thinking straight. "I just need some help getting you—"

"No!"

She looked down at his face. He aimed narrowed eyes at her, but his expression soon changed to one more somber.

"You have to leave me here," he said.

Julia shook her head. "No. Just let us move you, and we can make you more comfortable."

"There's no saving me."

Covering her mouth, Julia continued to cry. Ronald reached up and grabbed her arm to get her attention.

"This isn't your fault."

"Yes, it is. If I wouldn't have—"

"If I wouldn't have been so stubborn, none of this would have happened. It's not your fault, all right?"

Julia gave no response. She only cried harder.

Ronald looked up at Paul. He swallowed, his bloodshot eyes glassy.

"I'd like to go out into the woods, if possible."

Exhaling, Paul nodded. He hated this part more than anything in the world.

"Clear out the building with Katrina and Caleb and get everyone inside," Paul said to Keon.

"You sure you don't want me to come with you?"

"I got it. Just make sure there's no Demons in that place and get everyone inside."

Keon nodded. "You heard him. Everyone come on. Me, Katrina, and Caleb will make sure it's clear, and we'll gather inside."

The shocked group, many of whom were crying, trudged back up the short hill and followed Keon. The only one who remained was Julia. Paul put his hand on her shoulder.

"It's okay. Go ahead and join up with the others."

She glanced up at Paul, then down at Ronald again. Ronald nodded, smiling at her.

She cried as she walked away, not looking back.

"You going to be able to get up?" Paul asked.

"I think so."

Ronald rolled onto his side, gasping for air as he did. Paul kneeled down and helped him up to his feet. The shirt fell off of him, and he didn't bother to pick it back up. He held his crimson-stained hand over his wound, blood continuing to leak from it.

Paul walked with Ronald into the woods, keeping his eye out for other Demons.

"This is fine right here," Ronald said. He fell to a knee and Paul kneeled next to him.

"You all right?"

"It just hurts, man."

Paul clutched his shoulder. "It'll be all over soon."

Ronald sat against a tree. When he looked up at Paul, his eyes had turned an even darker shade of red.

Paul's stomach turned. He hated this job, but as leader of the group, it was his duty. He couldn't pass this burden on to anyone else.

"How do you want it?" Paul asked.

"Quick. I don't wanna feel nothing."

Paul nodded. If put in the same position as Ronald, that was the option he'd have chosen as well. It was the more comfortable option for him, too. Others who he'd had to euthanize hadn't wanted to face the blade. Suffocation was much worse on both parties.

He took a deep breath as he pulled the machete from its sheath. The blood of freshly slain Demons still dripped off of it.

"You don't have to wipe it down," Ronald said.

"It's out of respect." Paul pulled a rag from his back pocket and ran it across the blade, soaking up the blood. "Anything you wanna say?"

"Tell my wife and my boy that I love 'em. And tell 'em that I'm sorry that this happened. But don't tell 'em why it happened, if you don't mind. I don't want my wife thinking I died 'cause I was stubborn."

Paul nodded. "I'll be sure they know how much you love them, but I'm sure they already know that."

Tears welled from Ronald's eyes. "Take care of Brooke and your little one. That's the other thing you can do for me. Make sure you never leave 'em."

Paul cried now. The machete shook in his hand. He wasn't sure he could do this.

"I'm ready."

Ronald shut his eyes.

Paul's hands quaked harder as he raised the blade. He was sure he was going to miss if he kept his eyes shut, and he worried it would only make this more painful for Ronald.

"I'm sorry," Paul said as he opened his eyes.

He swung, and he didn't miss. The blade cut through Ronald's throat until it met the tree.

Paul turned away and threw up onto the ground. He went down to one knee, crying.

All he could think of was Ronald's wife and little boy. Of Brooke and their soon to be born child.

He wanted to have a home for them. To end all this.

35

THE WIND BRUSHED against the trees outside, and it was the only noise that could be heard from inside the building. Everyone sat in silence. Candles had been lit and illuminated the room enough to see the somber looks on everyone's faces. Outside, the moon hid behind the clouds.

Shell sat cross-legged on the dusty wooden floor with a small sack of berries on her lap. She stared at the ground instead of the food, trying not to eat the fruit too quickly. Keon and Katrina sat against the wall next to her. Keon ran his hand over the scruffy shadow of a three-day-old beard. When he looked over at Shell, she turned away.

Paul had settled into a chair on the other side of the room with his back turned to the group. While everyone else crowded around each other, Paul had separated himself. Shell wondered what he was thinking. She hadn't been told what had happened when they'd left Paul alone with Ronald, but it hadn't been difficult to figure out, and she'd come to her own conclusion. In the few instances when someone in town had been bitten, Lewis had made her go to her room while the situation had been handled.

But she'd always known what was happening. The same thing that had happened when Shell had only been a young girl and her horse, Coin, had broken her leg.

Shell tucked her berries back into her bag and pushed herself up to her feet.

"Where are you going?" Keon asked her in a whisper.

"To talk to Paul."

"Whoa," Keon said, reaching up and taking Shell by the wrist.

Shell's brow furrowed. "What?"

"You gotta just let him be. This is his way of coping with this shit."

Shell glanced back over to Paul. He was rubbing his face now, burying it into his hands.

"I can't just let him sit there by himself like that."

"It's what he wants," Keon said.

"Is that what you would want?" Shell asked him.

Keon thought about it for a moment, and then he shook his head. "But I know that's what he wants."

"Go talk to him," Katrina said to Shell.

Keon looked at his sister and shook his head.

"Maybe he doesn't wanna talk to *you* in these situations, because he thinks you're going to lecture him or something," Katrina said.

"What? You think that's how I talk to him?"

Katrina ignored her brother and said again to Shell, "Go talk to him."

Shell shook her head. "You two are something else."

"You just never had a sibling," Keon said.

Shell left her bag on the ground and made her way over to the other side of the single-room building. He didn't notice her when she arrived.

"Mind if I sit?" she asked.

Paul looked up from his hands. He cleared his throat and sat up straight, then wiped his face.

"Um, you know, I'd rath—"

"You look like you could use someone to talk to."

Shell sat down against the wall before Paul could say anything else. She faced him, her knees up to her chin. Paul ran his hand over his face and sighed.

"I don't know what you want me to say."

"There's nothing, in particular, I want you to say. This just isn't the Paul I've come to know."

"So you know me now, huh?"

"I know that this isn't you. I know that you're strong and that all these people lean on and depend on you."

"And that's just it. They depend on me. And why should they when all I do is let them down?"

"What happened today with Ronald wasn't your fault. He said as much. He made his own choice."

"But the choice to join us on this journey? That was me. He was only in this situation because of me."

Shell narrowed her eyes. "That's bullshit and you know it. Him being in that situation had nothing to do with you. All you're trying to do is keep everyone safe and protect your family."

"And what if I can't do that anymore? Keep everyone safe. My family safe."

Shell shook her head. "Like I said, that's not the Paul I know. It doesn't take much time around you to know how strong you are. How much you love your wife. Your unborn child."

Paul looked down at the ground and clasped his hands together.

"You know, the last thing Ronald said to me was to take care of his family. That was all he wanted. He was completely selfless in that way. Why do I get to live on, and he doesn't?"

"It's not your choice to decide who lives and who dies. The only thing you can do is try to help us all make the right decisions to try and survive."

"Yeah, well, I'm not exactly the best at making decisions. What kind of selfish prick gets his wife pregnant during the apocalypse? How am I supposed to keep a baby alive in this world?"

Shell stood up. "If you're afraid to live, then what's the point of any of this?"

She stared at him for a moment, studying his eyes. Then she walked back across the room to try and rest for the evening.

36

SHELL'S EYES opened as she gasped. She sat up and looked around the room. Candles continued to glow, as the sun had yet to come out, and everyone still lay in their bedrolls. Sweat rolled down her cheeks. Her hair was wet. She placed her hand over her heart and felt it racing. Then she put her palm over her eyes and breathed in heavily.

She'd had the dream again. The same one about seeing her family out in the yard of their house.

How do I stop having these dreams?

She lay down on her back and stared up at the ceiling, focusing on the orange glow of the candles dimly lighting the room. Closing her eyes, she focused on her breathing.

Shell's heart rate had just lowered to a manageable level when she heard something outside. Again, she sat up.

The wind blew hard outside, beating against the broken building.

It probably just knocked something over.

Another strange noise sounded out. Shell instinctively reached for her bow and quiver. Then she put her hand on

Keon's shoulder, waking him. He stirred, groaning, and finally opening his eyes.

"What is it?" he asked.

"I think someone's outside."

He woke up quicker after hearing that. He sat up and grabbed his crossbow, then sat in silence with Shell to listen.

"You're sure it's not just the wind?"

Shell shook her head. "I don't think so."

They went quiet again. Other than the wind, there was nothing.

"I think you're hearing things. The wind is playing tricks on you. Go back to sleep while we can—"

The door was busted open, and the sound of the aggressive wind was replaced by the collected snarls of a horde of Deads.

Shell jumped to her feet and nocked an arrow. She aimed toward the door and fired. She hit one of the Deads in the side of the neck, knocking it to the ground.

Yelling echoed through the building as the others in the group woke. Shell nocked another arrow, but the others blocked her shot as they began to stand, panicking. Then there were screams.

Deads fell on top of bodies near the door before the people could wake up fully. Between the screams and commotion, Shell heard the tearing flesh between the snarls.

"Help them!" someone yelled.

Caleb swung a bat at the creatures, but more continued to pour through the door. Shell watched a Dead fall on top of Caleb.

"Everyone, grab your weapons and fight!" Paul commanded. He swung his machete into a Dead's skull. "We've got to keep them out of here."

Shell aimed an arrow toward the door, but couldn't get a clean shot between all the people.

"It's not gonna work," Keon said. With his crossbow in hand, he ran for the door.

"Keon, wait!" Shell yelled.

But he didn't listen. He pushed between people until he got close to the door, then fired his crossbow point-blank into a Dead's temple.

Shell looked in the vicinity for anything she could use as a weapon. She happened along a board. Picking it up, she noticed a rusty nail protruding from one end of it.

This'll have to do.

She turned to head for the door and noticed Katrina pinned against a wall by a Dead. It snapped its jaws inches from her face as she tried to fight it off.

"Help!" she yelled.

Shell ran over to her and swung the board, driving the nail into the Dead's brain. It held onto Katrina for another moment before its grip loosened, and Katrina shoved it to the ground.

"Thanks," Katrina said.

Shell nodded, turning as she heard a scream. Lindsey, a single woman in her thirties who Shell had only talked to one brief time, had been taken down by a Dead, which was dining on her throat now.

At the back side of the room, Caleb had made it to his feet, having survived the previous creature that had taken him down. He wrestled with a long-haired Dead wearing coveralls. The creature had to weigh two hundred and fifty pounds, making it a tough match for the large Caleb. The Dead pushed Caleb against a wall. It then lunged its face at Caleb, who ducked out of the way. The Dead knocked over two candles.

Shell turned her attention to a creature coming at her. It extended its arms and she side-stepped it. Then she pulled an arrow from her quiver and drove it into the side of the monster's head. As it fell to the ground, she armed herself with another arrow and looked around for the next Dead to take down.

Orange flames rose from the floor as the back of the room became illuminated. The candles which had fallen had landed on something flammable. Scattered on the floor were Deads along with the few humans the creatures had killed. Several more Deads blocked the front door—the only way out of the burning building.

"We've got to clear these bastards out of the way and get the hell out of here," Paul said.

The world slowed around Shell. She saw the Deads tearing into humans on the ground. Others in the group screamed as they fought off the monsters. Shell had never been in a situation like this.

Hands grabbing onto her shoulders pulled her from her daze. Keon stood in front of her.

"We've gotta get out of here, now," he said. "Grab your shit and come on."

Looking around the room, Shell shook her head. "We can't just leave them here."

Keon looked back at the bodies on the ground. Then he glanced back at Shell.

"We don't have time. We've gotta go."

But Shell couldn't move. The surrounding death consumed her, taking her back to her town and when all her friends had died.

Keon pushed an oncoming Dead away, sending it across the room. It bumped into another Dead and they both fell to the ground.

"Shell! Come on!"

He grabbed Shell by the hand and pulled her toward the door. Aware of her surroundings again, Shell pulled her hand away and reached down to grab her gear. Then she hurried over to Keon. Together, they helped the last few remaining people in their group to get away from the Deads, and then joined the others outside.

Paul ran toward the door, ready to go back inside, but Keon stopped him.

"This is everyone."

"Are you sure?"

Keon nodded.

Shell moved a safe distance away from the building and then looked back at it. Flames licked at the air, which was filled with the scent of rotting flesh. Shell covered her mouth, trying to keep herself from puking. She heard a grotesque snarl then and glanced back to the building

A Dead had walked out the door, its body engulfed in flames.

When she saw the creature, all Shell could think of were the dead humans inside. Her look of disgust turned to anger. She stood up straight, drawing an arrow from her quiver and nocking it into her bow. She pulled back and aimed at the flaming creature.

"Smile, you bastard."

She let go and the arrow landed between the Dead's eyes. It fell onto its back and stared straight at the sky, the arrow protruding from its face like a grave marker.

Inside, the last few remaining Deads were surely looking for the exit. There were no human screams.

"We've gotta move," Paul said.

He started jogging away and the others followed. Keon waited for Shell.

"Come on," he said.

Shell took one last look at the burning Deads exiting the building and thought of those who'd perished inside. Then she joined Keon and they jogged away, catching up to the others in what remained of their group.

37

PAUL WASN'T sure how far they'd walked, but it had to have at least been a mile and a half. He'd kept his focus forward and hadn't looked back. Dawn had arrived, but other than that he'd been oblivious to his surroundings. He'd barely noticed the ache that had built up in his legs from all the walking, ignoring it as he worked to get as far away from the burning building as possible.

"Paul, I think we've gone far enough," a male voice said from behind him.

Paul stopped, unaware of who had even been speaking. He turned around for the first time since leaving the building. The remaining members of the group stood ten yards away, staring back at him. His throat was dry, and he breathed heavily.

He fell down to one knee.

"Paul!" Keon said, running toward him.

Hands touched either side of his back as Keon kneeled at one side of him and Katrina the other.

"Give him some space," Katrina said to the others who'd approached to see if he was okay.

Paul heaved for air.

"Let's help him over to that rock," Keon said.

They each took Paul under an arm and helped him to his feet. Holding him up, they led him to a large rock at the nearby tree line. They set him down onto it, and Keon squatted in front of him.

"You all right, brother?"

Paul stared blankly into Keon's eyes.

"Paul?"

Paul gagged, then leaned over the side of the rock and vomited onto the ground. People in the group gasped and Keon put his arm around Paul again.

Wiping his mouth, Paul stood up. Keon tried to stop him, but Paul pushed his friend's hand away. He walked away from the rock, catching his breath. Once he'd calmed himself down, he turned to the group.

Everyone stared at him. He knew the look on their faces. These people looked to him for guidance, for leadership. And, once again, he'd failed them. Unable to look at them any longer, Paul turned around even before he got around to speaking.

"Hey, dude," Keon said, approaching. He spoke low enough to where only Paul could hear. "You okay?"

Staring back at his friend, Paul narrowed his eyes. He shook his head.

"No, I'm not okay." He spoke loud enough to where everyone could hear, and he sidestepped Keon to address the whole group. "What the hell are we doing out here?"

"What do you mean?" Caleb asked.

Paul pointed down the path from which they'd come. "Look at what happened back there. How many people did we lose?"

Everyone stared at him. No one answered. Paul glanced back at Keon.

"How many?" he asked, raising his voice and demanding an answer to a question he already knew.

Keon looked away, putting his hands on his hips. "Four."

Paul focused on the group again. "Four. Four more people dead. Dead under my leadership. And all because I thought that we could walk out here and take back some land from a bunch of thugs who have no reason for being there. But how the hell are we supposed to do that if I can't even keep us safe from a bunch of brainless monsters?"

"You're putting too much pressure on yourself, man. Why don't you step over here and—"

"And what?" Paul turned to Keon again. "Calm down? Is that what you were gonna say?"

Again, Keon averted his friend's gaze.

"You can't put all the blame for this on yourself," a female voice said.

Paul turned to see Shell had stepped out from the group.

"These people don't aimlessly follow you. They're with you because they believe in you. And I saw firsthand exactly why they do when you told me you wanted to come and take back my town. Because of the passion you have and how selfless you are. It isn't just your family you want to protect. You want to make life better for everyone here, and people believe that. *I* believe that." Shell approached Paul, stopping only a few feet in front of him. "Those people who died back there didn't die because you made them come along with you. They died because they believed in you and knew that you were only trying to make their lives better. None of us are here because we have to be."

"She's right," Katrina said. "Shit, we'd all be lost without you around."

Keon placed his hand on Paul's shoulder. "Seriously, brother. You bear a lot of burdens for all of us, and you're one hell of a leader. We'd follow you into hell if we had to. Wouldn't we?"

The group gave a mixed response of "Yeahs" and "Hell yeahs."

When they fell silent again, Shell said, "I chose to stay with you all because I believed you when you told me we could get my home back. I believed *in* you. And there's no way in hell we're turning around now. Not after all we've been through and how close we are."

Paul scanned everyone's faces. Shell was right. They did believe in him. Though they were broken, sad, and beaten, everyone was still there, standing alongside him. Bailing out now would only be disrespectful to those who had perished. He looked at Keon, and then back at Shell.

"What the hell are we all just standing around for, then?" Paul asked. "We've got a town to take back!"

Everyone raised their fists and hollered. Paul turned and wrapped his arm around his friend Keon, and they started down the train tracks again, moving on toward Yazoo City.

38

BY THE MIDDLE of the next afternoon, the group moved along the tracks like the Demons they worked to avoid. They dragged their legs, hunching over their limp bodies. Paul knew the constant moving from place to place had taken its toll on them. The train tracks were out in the open now, and the flat landscape provided little escape from the sun's rays. He looked back at the tired and hungry group. It was clear they were in no shape to fight. They would reach Yazoo City soon, and he wanted to attack the gang some time the following day, but that was only if they got there with enough time to find food and to rest. Going into the town before everyone had had the chance to recharge would only lead to a slaughter.

He swung his backpack off his shoulder, dropping it to the ground. "Let's rest here for ten minutes."

A collective sigh passed through the group, and their bags hit the ground almost in chorus. The only one not to drop her things was Shell. She walked away from the group and past Paul, finishing the climb up the short hill. Using her hand as a visor from the sun, she stared into the distance. When she turned around, a smile stretched across her face.

"What is it?" Paul asked.

Shell gestured for him to join her.

Paul jogged over to her and looked out over the hill himself. About a mile down the tracks, he could see buildings. They were much shorter than the ones in Jackson, but it was clear there was a town ahead.

"That's downtown Yazoo," Shell said. "Well, if you want to call it that."

"How far is your house from here?"

"A mile or so away once we get on the other side of town."

Keon and Katrina approached.

"That's your town?" Keon asked.

Shell nodded.

"Thank God," Katrina said. "We should keep going and get there while we've still got sunlight."

"Hold on," Paul said. "I know we're all tired and anxious, but we've got to think about this a little bit. If we had a whole town to ourselves, where would we be?"

Katrina's expression turned sour.

"He's right," Keon said to his sister. "No way we wouldn't search every inch of those buildings in town."

"I did that a long time ago," Shell said. "Surely, they'll know that's why my house was so well-stocked. If I had to guess, they're probably going to be staying close to there."

"I wouldn't go assuming that," Paul said. "If I were to take a guess, I'd say they're still going to look. Honestly, I would. Either way, we can't afford to risk it. We're gonna have to walk around the downtown area to avoid it."

"How much time is that going to add?" Katrina asked.

"Probably at least an hour," Shell said.

"Well worth it," Paul said. "I know everyone is exhausted, but it's what we've got to do to stay safe. I'm not losing anyone else over being careless. And we can't relinquish our element of surprise because that's how we're going to take those bastards down."

"All right," Katrina said. "I'll go ahead and let the others know we're going to get moving again. If we're going to lose an hour, we need to move. We need to find a place to stay close to town so we can go to Shell's house early in the morning."

Paul nodded, then turned back to Shell. "Do you know of anywhere we can stay the night?"

"I've got a few ideas. We should head around on the east side of town. There's some houses and buildings over there for us to choose from, and I don't think it's anywhere that gang would be hanging around."

They departed only a few minutes after that. Most in the group remained positive, happy that they were close to their destination. But Paul could feel a sense of nervousness amongst everyone. Being closer to the town meant being closer to war.

With a couple of hours of daylight left, they found a building east of town. It had once been a church, its white steeple still in place on top, though it had faded to a dull gray. Nevertheless, the structure was in good enough shape to offer shelter for the night. Paul allowed everyone to get settled in before informing the group of his next move. He stepped up onto the stage at the front of the room and looked out over everyone.

"I know you're all tired and exhausted, and you'll have your rest tonight. We're all going to need it because tomorrow is the day we've been waiting forever for since we lost our home in Georgia. But before we get there, a few things need to happen.

"We need sufficient food for the evening. There's a lot of open country in the area, which means there's a good chance of finding something to eat. A deer would be nice, but there should at least be some squirrels or foxes around. Caleb, I'm going to leave you in charge of hunting. You should take someone along with you."

"I'll go," Keon said.

Paul shook his head. "You're coming with me."

"Where?"

"We're going to go to Shell's house tonight."

Chatter spread among the group. Paul raised his hands, then whistled to get everyone's attention back on him.

"We can't just march on in there tomorrow with no plan," Paul said. "Shell can draw us a map, sure, but that won't help us with knowing how many people we're up against. So, we're going to go there tonight and scope the place out." He looked at Keon, then at Shell. "Are you two all right with that?"

They looked at each other, then nodded. Paul returned the gesture.

"Good. We'll leave once the sun goes down, then we can sneak over there without being seen. In the meantime, let's all continue getting settled in and hope that Caleb can catch us something to eat."

The group spread out and Paul stepped off the stage. He found a place to be alone for a while where he could think of his wife, and pray that the night went well, putting him one step closer to being reunited with her.

39

SHELL'S HEART beat faster as they got closer to her home. The sun had gone down, but she'd traveled these roads and fields so many times that having no light was no issue for her. They stayed low, hiding in the tall grass and behind buildings, trees, and the metal remains of vehicles. Even with a light breeze, she couldn't help sweating, and felt over-heated due to her nerves. At any turn, they could come across members of the gang roaming the town, or a herd of Deads. A fight with Deads could bring the attention of the gang, so Paul had advised they avoid any confrontation with them if they could.

When they reached the top of a hill near her house, Shell lay down on her belly. She signaled to Keon and Paul to join her. Then she crawled the few feet up to look over the top of the slope.

"There it is," she said.

A giant bonfire illuminated the front yard of Shell's farmhouse. Torches had been lit around the yard, as well. A group sat around the campfire, conversing with each other and laughing. Several others walked around nearby. Shell saw two people harvesting crops from her vegetable garden. She pulled back, shifting onto her back and lying out of sight, and Paul and Keon followed suit.

"There has to be at least twenty of them," Keon said. "How the hell are we supposed to face all of them with the numbers we've got?"

"They might have numbers, but we'll have the element of surprise," Paul said. "The right strategy can trump numbers. Didn't you ever read about the Romans?"

Keon shook his head, smiling, and then turned to Shell. "This place is exactly as you said it was."

"It is," Paul said. "And it's absolutely worth us fighting for it."

Shell remained silent as the two men talked. A surreal feeling had come over her. When she had begun traveling with Dylan, he'd helped her quickly realize that her home was gone and that she would not be returning there. Now that she was back and saw the raiders who'd overtaken it yanking her crops out of the ground and laughing and having a good time in front of her house, the violated feeling she'd had when they'd thrown her into the barn returned. She felt sad, angry, and even ashamed. She'd let her parents and Lewis down. She knew their graves lay on the other side of her house, and she couldn't bare letting these men parade around her home with her lost loved ones nearby.

She breathed, trying to push aside all the emotions flowing through her. She needed to be focused if she wanted to help get the town back.

The scream of a goat struck her ears, and Shell's eyes opened wide. She turned over onto her belly and crawled up the hill again.

Two men had Lisa, her goat, out of the barn and in the open. Lisa looked confused, running in circles and crying out. One of the men tilted his head to the sky, pressing a metal container to his lips and downing a liquid. He wiped his mouth, then frowned as he brought his leg back and kicked the goat in the stomach.

The goat cried out.

The man said something, then kicked Lisa again.

Shell's eyes glassed over. She clenched her fist and snorted like a bull. Reaching for her quiver, she removed an arrow and sat up to load it into her bow. Keon and Paul grabbed her from either side.

"Let me go!" she said.

"Stop," Keon said, trying to quiet her down. He and Paul pulled her out of sight and held her down on her back.

Shell kicked her legs out at them before letting the tears flow. The goat screamed again as the men laughed. Shell quit struggling and pushed Keon and Paul's hands off of her. She ran her arm across her eyes.

"It's not going to do any of us any good if you act on that emotion now," Keon said. "Save it and bring it with you tomorrow."

"He's right," Paul said. "You need to—"

"I get it," Shell said, cutting him off. She wiped the rest of the tears from her eyes.

She slid down the hill and started back the way they'd come.

Shell didn't care how outnumbered they were. She was coming back to her home, and she was taking it back from the bastards who'd stolen it from her.

40

ON THE WAY back to camp, Shell said nothing. Paul and Keon talked some, but they stayed mostly silent, as well. All Shell could think about was how much she wanted to kill every one of the people who'd stolen her home from her. She'd never been one to think that way, but the town was her home, and these men had stolen it from her. Her family had kept it as a peaceful place of refuge for years, and Shell had done the same for several more after everyone else had passed. Those thugs had no right to be there, and she was going to be sure they knew that—especially the two men she'd seen senselessly abusing Lisa.

As they approached the building where they'd made camp for the evening, the front door opened. Not one person had taken rest. They'd all stayed awake, waiting for Shell, Paul, and Keon to return. Most in the group stood as they walked through the door.

Caleb and Katrina moved to the front of the group. Katrina hugged her brother, then Paul.

"Glad to see y'all made it back," Caleb said. "We were starting to get worried."

"What'd you find out?" Katrina asked.

"The place is every bit as beautiful as she described it," Keon said, looking over at Shell.

"Beautiful farmhouse. Plenty of land to plant crops. Animals. There's other houses nearby, too. Plenty of places for all of us to live. The town seems to be in pretty immaculate shape."

A glow spread through the crowd. Everyone smiled and conversed with each other.

"It's not all rainbows, y'all," Paul said. Everyone went quiet and focused back on him.

"Dylan was right," Keon said. "There's a whole hell of a lot of them. Got us well outnumbered from what we could tell."

"So, what are you trying to tell us?" Martin asked.

Paul put his hands on his hips and stared at the ground. He looked up and scanned everyone's faces.

"This isn't going to be just my decision. I can't hold that burden anymore. You all have to decide for yourselves if this is what you want. As much as I want to think otherwise, it's unlikely we all make it out of this fight alive. It's your lives, and you've gotta choose how you want to live them."

Shell looked around the room. The people seemed tired, broken. No one spoke aloud, but their faces said everything.

Julia grabbed her bag and stepped forward. "I don't think we should do it. In fact, I think we should leave tonight and head back."

"Same here," Jesse said.

Two more people came forward, nodding in agreement.

Julia said, "We can find somewhere else to make our home. This doesn't seem worth it. We've already lost enough on this trip."

"This is our best shot at settling somewhere," Martin

said. "Nowhere we have found since leaving Georgia has been sustainable. I'm tired of running."

"Then you go in there and get yourself killed!" Jesse said. "I ain't doing it!"

An argument broke out between the opposing sides. Shell felt her heart rate increasing. A tingling feeling ran down her arms, and she began to sweat. She balled her fist, then stepped forward.

"Stop it!"

The room went silent and looked her way.

"I know you're all scared," she said. "I am, too. If I wasn't scared, I wouldn't have run away from my home in the first place. I would have stayed there, and I'd likely be dead now. Now I know a lot of you think that I only want your help so I can get my farmhouse back. And yes, that is part of the reason why. It's my home. But the fact is, it can be *our* home. We can all live in the town together and bring some normalcy back into our lives. We can stop running, and we can *live*."

Shell walked over to Julia. "You said you all can just keep traveling and find somewhere else. That might be true, but if it were so easy, then why haven't you found anywhere yet? Do you think you're just going to stumble upon a place that's going to be perfect?"

Julia breathed slowly, staring into Shell's eyes but saying nothing. Shell looked around the room.

"Did we really come all this way just to turn around and go back to square one? No matter where we go, it's going to be hard. There's going to be a fight, and there are no guarantees. But I can tell you that I lived here for my entire life with almost no incidents until these bastards came and took my home away from me. We can do more than survive here. We can make lives for ourselves. Real, enjoyable lives. Is that not worth fighting for?"

Everyone looked at each other as the room fell silent. Shell's words hung in the air. Shell was ready to fight, but knew it would be impossible on her own. She needed these people at her side. She wanted them with her, to start a new life together.

Julia looked at the others in her newly formed group, and a smile formed on her face as she looked at Shell and nodded. Jesse did the same.

"We're with you," Julia said.

The room erupted, and there was new energy.

Paul and Keon looked at Shell, smiles across their faces. Shell returned the looks with a grin of her own.

We just might have a chance after all.

41

As the sun poured in through the windows, Shell sat in the corner with her arms over her knees. She hadn't slept much the night before. None of them had. The room had remained silent all through the night, without even one person snoring or breathing loudly. Everyone was scared, and they all knew they'd have plenty of time to sleep whether they succeeded or failed.

Shell had passed some time that morning by taking a white shirt she had in her bag and tearing a piece of it off. She'd pulled out a pen and covered the piece of cloth with names. Those of every person who had lived in the town with her. In the center were the three loved ones dearest to her: her parents and Lewis. She looked over all the names, and they were a reminder of the legacy she had to protect by getting the town back from those bandits.

She wrapped the cloth around her forearm and tied it. She'd positioned it where the three most important names stared at her. They would bring her strength during the fight.

Others in the room began to stir, but no one spoke.

While everyone checked their gear, Shell quietly waited. She'd counted her sixteen arrows as many times. Her bowstring was set, the crosshairs calibrated. She was ready.

Paul opened his eyes, and Shell saw determination and focus in them. He stood up, and everyone watched him as he walked to the middle of the room. He scanned everyone's faces.

"Today is our day. Let's go take it."

Everyone raised their weapons into the air and cheered as they stood. Everyone but Shell. She didn't smile. Didn't cheer. In her mind, there wasn't anything to cheer about until every member of that gang had been put down.

She grabbed her things and stood. As she threw her bag and quiver over one shoulder, she felt a hand grab her other.

"Are you ready for this?" Keon asked.

"Are you?"

He smiled. "I feel a lot better having you on my side."

She could see his hand shaking. She took it and squeezed. They stared into each other's eyes, and the trembling in his hand calmed. There were no words to be said. Shell leaned in and kissed Keon on the cheek. The shake in his hand faded entirely with that, and he smiled.

Everyone exited the building, leaving Paul, Keon, and Shell as the last three people inside. Paul extended his hand to the door, offering to let Shell walk out before him.

"This is your show. Lead the way."

With focused eyes, Shell went outside. The others all stared at her. Paul and Keon walked past her and joined the rest of the group. Shell looked into all of their faces. They were waiting for her to lead.

She nodded and stepped onto the road. She headed in the direction of her house, and everyone followed.

THEY ARRIVED at the Holstead farm, a quarter-mile away from Shell's. It was the rendezvous point she, Paul, and Keon had decided on the previous evening.

"We'll split into our three teams here," Paul said. "My squad will go at the house from the east, Keon's from the north, and Shell's from the west. We'll surround them and hit 'em with everything we've got."

Shell's group held Martin, Julia, and Trent. They'd been chosen to go with her because the west side of the house required the most travel from the Holstead farm, and these three were the most athletic in the group. They'd be able to move faster and stealthier through the rural farmlands to reach the west side of Shell's house.

"Only bring your essentials," Paul said. "We'll leave everything else here at this house and come back and get it when all this is over."

"There's a shed in back we'll keep everything in," Keon said.

They walked to the shed and everyone dropped the gear they didn't need inside.

Shell left the few things in her bag that weren't essential. She only needed to pull out her extra clothes and a few other non-essentials. Everything else, she needed with her, including water, a small assortment of first aid items, and some nuts and berries. The bag she kept was small enough to where she could carry it with her without slowing her down or impairing her in combat. When she'd finished, she stepped away from the shed and waited for the others in her squad to finish unloading stuff. Keon noticed her and walked over. He had his hands on his hips and looked back for a moment before putting his eyes on her again.

"Listen, I know you're the last person who needs to hear this, but take care of yourself out there. I'd like to see you on the other side of this."

"You will. I look forward to it."

Keon smiled and looked into her eyes again. He leaned in, cupped her face, and kissed her on the lips.

Shell's eyes were wide as they kissed, but she didn't pull back. She put her arms around him, her hands landing on his shoulder blades. She closed her eyes and relaxed, kissing him more passionately. When it was over, they pulled away and stared at each other without saying anything.

"About fucking time," Paul said.

Shell and Keon turned to see everyone else in the group looking at them. Shell moved her hair out of her face and blushed, her arms still wrapped around Keon.

"I was starting to wonder if you even liked women anymore," Katrina said to her brother. "'Bout time you grew the balls to do that."

Keon laughed. "The hell with both of you."

"Not today, friend," Paul said. "Now, you two finish up so we can move out."

The rest of the group went back to what they'd been doing, giving Shell and Keon some privacy.

"That was a little awkward," Shell said.

"Sorry about that."

"No, it's okay. I'm just a little curious about what *did* take you so long, like Katrina said." Shell grinned.

"Now don't go all acting like that."

Shell grabbed his face and kissed him again. "I'm picking on you. Just take care of yourself, all right? I really would like to see you on the other side of this."

"I'll be there. Don't you worry."

"All right, everyone group up."

Shell and Keon held hands until they'd moved too far apart, letting go. Shell stood with Martin, Julia, and Trent.

"Y'all ready?" she asked.

All three nodded. She saw the fear in their eyes. She was scared, too, but refused to show it.

"We'll have to move fast since we have the furthest to go. We don't want the others waiting on us too long. Everyone okay with that?"

"I'm here to do what needs to be done," Trent said.

"I'm just tired of running away," Julia said. "If this place is as great as you say it is, then hell yes I'm okay with it."

"Same," Martin said.

Shell grinned and nodded.

"Good luck, everyone," Paul said. "Remember the signals. And once everyone is in position, raise hell."

Everyone in the crowd cheered. Shell looked over to see Keon smile and nod at her. She returned the gesture, adding a wink.

"See you on the other side," Paul said.

42

SHELL'S HEART raced as her farmhouse came into view. They were several hundred yards away still, but the open farm-land gave a clear look at her home. Sweat seeped from her pores, and seeing her home only angered her and caused her to perspire more. She took a deep breath and refocused.

"Stay low," she said to the others.

They were far enough away to where they'd be difficult to see from her house, but Shell wasn't willing to take any chances. The overgrown grass hid them if they stayed low, and so she decided they might as well take advantage of it. Her squad was making good time, anyway, and she predicted they'd be in position near the same time as the other two groups led by Paul and Keon.

She was busy looking off at the farmhouse when she heard a noise coming from her right.

A group of four Deads lumbered by about twenty yards away, emerging from behind an abandoned piece of farm equipment.

"Get down!" she said, diving to the ground.

The other three dived down beside her. They were quiet, listening to the snarling foursome.

"I counted four of them," Shell said. "Did any of you see any others?"

"I think there were just four," Martin said.

"What are we going to do?" Julia asked. "This is a pretty open field, and they're far enough away from us where we should be able to outrun them."

"I'm not worried about outrunning them," Shell said. "I'm worried about them drawing attention to us. I know we're still pretty far away from the house, but it's quiet out here. Once those things see us, they're only going to snarl louder, and that could carry quite a distance."

"We can't just wait here for them to leave," Trent said. "The others are—"

"Waiting on us, I know," Shell said, cutting him off.

She thought of what they could do, and only one answer came to her mind.

"We're going to have to sneak over there and take them out."

"That's just going to waste time," Julia said.

"Do you have any other ideas?" Shell asked. "Waiting for them to leave is going to waste much more time."

"Yeah, I have an idea. We run like hell."

"Shell's right, though," Martin said. "What if they make enough noise to attract the people who are there? Then we put everyone in danger."

"Taking those things down is just as risky," Julia said.

"I didn't say it wasn't risky," Shell said. "But we don't have a lot of options. That's the one I think is best."

"I agree," Martin said. He looked at Trent, and so did the others.

Trent's eyes glanced around before settling on Julia. He sighed.

"Sorry, Julia."

Julia exhaled, then shrugged. "It's fine. Let's get this over with."

She pushed herself up onto her knees, but Shell put her hand on her back and urged her back down.

"We can't just up and run over there. Let's use this tall grass to our advantage. We can sneak behind that tractor and draw them out of sight from the house. Then we'll take them down."

"That sounds good," Martin said. "We'll follow your lead."

Shell nodded, then crawled on her belly toward the small pack of Deads. She tried making the least amount of noise possible but was confident that the rustling of the grass wouldn't be enough to garner the attention of the dumb creatures. They made it to the back side of the tractor, the Deads lumbering on the other side of it.

Reaching behind her, Shell prepared an arrow. The others nodded at her as they grabbed their weapons.

"Now!"

Shell jumped up, nocking the arrow into her bow. She aimed and let go of the bowstring, landing an arrow in the back of her target's head.

Trent, who also used a bow, took a shot at one of the other creatures. He missed its head, landing the arrow in its shoulder. It distracted the creature long enough for Martin to rush over to it and bury his hatchet into its head. Julia took down one of the creatures with her machete, and Martin killed the other with his hatchet. The whole ambush lasted only around thirty seconds.

When it was over, Shell lowered her bow and breathed

heavily, the adrenaline rushing through her body. Julia turned her way. Blood had splashed onto her face, and she squinted her eyes. Martin looked Shell's way, too. Only, like Julia, he wasn't looking at Shell, but beyond her.

Shell turned around.

A man sat on a horse, about thirty yards away from them. He had blonde hair, and he looked at Shell with wide eyes. She recognized him. It was Cody, the twenty-something-year-old who Ray had sent away to tell the rest of their gang about the town.

"Oh, shit," she said.

She drew an arrow and nocked it into her bow. The bandit took off. Shell let the arrow fly from her shaking bow, her hands quaking. The arrow missed by ten feet or more.

The man looked back as he rode, kicking the horse to go faster.

He was too far out of distance for her to shoot again.

And he was heading back toward Shell's house.

Shell clutched her chest, almost falling.

They'd lost the element of surprise.

43

PAUL LICKED his lips as he kneeled down behind the rusted vehicle. He had taken his squad to the next house over from Shell's. Several dozen acres separated the two homes, giving them some needed distance. He peeked over the hood. He could count seven men scattered around the yard, and another two sitting in rocking chairs on the front porch of the house. Just as Shell had predicted, the men were hanging around her house where she had gathered supplies and resources.

We've got you bastards.

Lowering his head, Paul sat with his back against the car.

"Get a good look at how many of them there are?" Tim asked.

"I counted nine, but there's gotta be more. They're probably in the house or the barn."

"They could be away from the house, too," Caleb said. "Out searching the town. That could be good."

"Yes, it could," Paul said.

That was the scenario Paul had hoped for. If at least some of the gang were away, scavenging the small town or off hunting, then they would have far fewer people to worry about taking out in the initial attack. Once they were gone, Paul and the others could hide until the other bandits returned, and then they could ambush them.

"So, what's the plan now?" Stewart asked.

"We'll have to wait for the others to get into position and give their signals," Paul said. "I'm gonna poke my head up again and see."

Paul shifted positions onto his knees and looked over the hood of the car again. He raised the binoculars to his face and then glanced to the north, where Keon had been directed to take his crew. He scanned the horizon until he saw a white flag sticking out of the ground next to the remains of a pickup truck. Then Keon poked his head out and looked in Paul's direction. He gave a thumbs-up, then hid behind the truck again.

"Keon's in position," Paul said to the others. "Now I've gotta look for Shell."

Paul looked into the binoculars again and pointed them west. He was looking straight across the yard and couldn't help but study the faces of the men he would be trying to kill in mere minutes. Then he focused beyond them and tried to find Shell, Martin, Julia, and Trent. He looked for their white flag next to every barrier but didn't see it.

They'd had plenty of time to get over there. Where were they?

The binoculars focused on the men on the front porch of Shell's farmhouse. They'd stood up from the rocking chairs and were staring at the south side of the property. As Paul moved the binoculars across the landscape, he saw the other bandits looking south, as well. Then he heard the horse, and the man yelling. He scanned the area until he saw the man on the horse, kicking its side as the animal barreled toward the house.

"What the hell is that?" Caleb asked. He got beside Paul and looked over the hood.

Paul put down the binoculars to watch the scene unfold with his own eyes. The man rode the horse into the middle of the yard, where five of the other men stood. He brought the horse to a stop several feet from them. Then he waved his arms and spoke loudly, but not enough to where Paul could hear him. He pointed in the direction from which he'd come. The same direction Shell's group were supposed to have approached the house from.

"Oh, shit," Paul said.

Paul's heart raced. He wasn't sure what to do. Shell and her squad had been outed, but the rest of them hadn't. The second they went to help Shell, though, they would be. But he couldn't let them go after her, Martin, Julia, and Trent.

The men drew blades ranging in size, and took off running toward where the man on the horse had been pointing. And the man on the horse kicked the animal and took off after them.

"Shit, Paul. What are we going to do?" Caleb asked.

But Paul didn't have to decide.

He heard the scream, and he looked north.

And saw his best friend running toward the men on the property.

"Goddammit, Keon."

Paul bit his lip, drawing blood. He drew his machete and raised it into the air. Caleb, Stewart, and Tim all stood beside him.

They ran toward the house.

44

SHELL DIDN'T KNOW what to do.

She stood behind the tractor, her heart racing. The man on the horse had sped away because he was outnumbered. But he had clearly recognized Shell, as she had him. He'd soon be back with others, and the fight would be over before it even started. Paul, Keon, and the others wouldn't stand a chance if Shell and her crew were taken out.

"We've got to head back," Julia said. "It's the only chance we've got."

"I'm with her," Trent said.

"No way," Martin said. "We can't."

"Why not?" Julia asked. "That guy's going to come back here with a hell of a lot more people, and they're going to kill us!"

"And you don't think they'll catch us?" Martin asked. "We're in the middle of an open field. There's no way we'll get away from them, especially if they all have horses."

The three continued to argue as panicking thoughts ran around in Shell's head. She massaged her right temple, feeling the veins pulsate. Then she turned to the others.

"Everyone, stop it!"

They looked at her. Sweat collected around her palm where she held her bow, and she clutched her other hand tight into a fist.

"We aren't leaving. Paul and Keon wouldn't leave us, so we're not hanging them out to dry. We came here to fight, and just because everything hasn't gone as planned doesn't mean we're going to run away and give up."

Shell drew an arrow from her quiver and readied it in her bow. Then she turned away from the others and walked around the other side of the tractor and faced the house. She squinted her eyes.

"Son of a bitch."

She watched as Keon and his squad ran towards the center of the yard. Then, moments later, Paul led his group. They'd been forced to initiate the attack early, and it was all her fault.

The others came to her side, but right as they got there, she returned the arrow to her quiver and started running.

"Shell, wait!" Martin yelled.

But she didn't. Couldn't. The plan had blown up because of her. If she had ignored the horde of Deads, she might have noticed the man on the horse.

She pumped her arms and ran.

She had to get to the house and help her friends before it was too late.

PAUL FOCUSED his attention on a man with a shadow of a beard who was wearing a backward, faded baseball cap. He appeared to be in his mid-40s. Was he a husband like Paul, or even a father? It didn't matter now. The man held up a large knife, aiming it at his oncoming assailant —Paul.

As Paul ran at the man in the ballcap, he watched Keon's squad arrive and begin the fight. Keon took down the first bandit he saw with his crossbow, hitting the man in the leg. Katrina ran up to the fallen bandit and slashed his throat as he stood up, bringing the first kill to the battle.

The man in the baseball cap yelled out as he ran at Paul. Paul raised the machete over his head and swung. The man rolled, avoiding the blow. The swing of the machete nearly sent Paul to the ground, too. Another bandit came at him with a knife, hoping to catch him off guard, but Paul swung the machete at the man's arm, driving the blade halfway through his wrist. The man screamed out, dropping the knife to the ground. Paul then drove the tip of the machete into the man's belly. Blood spewed from the bandit's mouth and he looked at Paul with pale eyes.

Before Paul could withdraw the blade from the dying man's gut, he heard a yell behind him. Baseball Cap lunged at Paul with the knife and Paul kicked backward, landing his boot into the man's gut. Baseball Cap doubled over and coughed, giving Paul enough time to get the machete out of the dead man's stomach. Paul's first victim fell to the ground. Paul raised the machete over his head to bring it down onto Baseball Cap, but Baseball Cap managed a swing of the knife. It slashed Paul across his side, cutting open his shirt. Paul yelled out in pain, nearly dropping the machete to the ground as he clutched his side. He raised his hand off the wound to see the blood.

With his head still down, Baseball Cap barreled his shoulder into Paul, sending him to the ground and causing him to drop the machete. The back of Paul's head hit the dirt, briefly disorienting him and sending a sharp pain to his skull. He looked over and saw his machete lying next to him. His wedding ring had come off during the fall, too, and lay near the machete. He reached out to grab it, but a tennis shoe slammed down on his hand. Paul screamed as Baseball Cap shifted more weight down onto his palm. Keeping his foot on Paul's hand, Baseball Cap kneeled and grabbed the machete and the ring. He laughed as he looked down at Paul.

"Maybe I'll find her and fuck 'er when you're dead."

Paul's eyes went wide as the man grinned and lifted the machete with both hands over his head.

"Sweet dreams, mother—"

An arrow pierced his throat from the back of his neck. Blood spilled out of each side of the wound like a fountain. Baseball Cap dropped the machete and it stuck in the dirt. Breathing heavily, Paul sat up.

Shell stood twenty yards away, her bow still aimed at where Baseball Cap had been standing. She hurried over and kneeled next to Paul.

"You all right?"

"Fine," Paul said, his eyes still wide.

"You're bleeding."

"I'll be fine," Paul said, retrieving his wedding ring and then pushing himself up.

He grabbed his machete and looked at the fight going on. He watched a large man stab Jesse in the arm, then topple on top of him and stab him again.

"Shit," Paul said. "We can't waste any more time."

He ran back into the fight.

45

SHELL WATCHED Paul race over to where Jesse had been taken down, all the while deciding on what her next move would be. She scanned the area and saw most of her people still standing, paired up with members of the gang and fighting. Paul and Keon had been able to maintain some surprise and take out a few of the bandits before the fight officially began, making the fight more even now.

But as she looked around the yard now, she couldn't find Keon. She searched amongst the fights, having seen him only moments earlier, but now he was gone.

A scream pulled her away, and she looked to her right to see a man strike Katrina in the face with the back of his hand. Katrina hit the ground and the man laughed. He held a spear as a weapon and pointed it at her.

Shell drew an arrow from her quiver and loaded it into her bow. She whistled, hoping it would draw the man's attention and buy her more time.

It worked.

The man looked her way as she pulled back the

bowstring. She let go and the arrow soared, catching the man in his left shoulder. He cried out and fell to the ground.

Shell ran over and found Katrina lying on the ground, gasping for air. She looked down at the man who she'd shot with the arrow and he wasn't moving. The shot had been perfect, piercing his heart and ending his life. Shell kneeled down by Katrina and checked her body for wounds, but found none aside from the blood oozing out of her nose from the man striking her.

"You all right?" Shell asked.

"Yeah," Katrina said.

Shell extended her hand and, when Katrina grabbed it, she pulled her up to her feet.

"Have you seen your brother?"

Katrina looked past Shell to glance around the property. "No. We were supposed to stay together, but that plan faded quick."

Shell brushed her aside and walked past her.

"Where are you going?" Katrina asked.

"To find him. Take care of yourself and I'll see you on the other side."

Shell stayed on the outskirts of all the fighting as she looked for Keon. She kept an arrow notched in her bow, looking for a shot to help her friends, but one never came. Each fight had the combatants too close together, and they were moving so fast that Shell risked hitting one of her friends instead of saving them.

A faint cry came from the barn, jerking away Shell's attention. It sounded familiar.

It sounded like Keon.

Shell lowered her bow so she could move faster, still keeping ahold of the arrow she'd held ready.

The barn doors stood ajar, and she opened them slowly

in case one of the gang members was inside waiting. Instead, all she saw was Keon, lying against the far wall and clutching his knee. Shell hurried over to him.

"Get out of here, Shell! It's a trap!"

Shell turned around, and she faced a man much larger than she was.

It was Cody.

He grabbed onto the wrist of her hand holding the bow and twisted. She cried out, dropping her bow and the arrow to the ground. He then used his other hand to push her down. She landed on her ass, her bow lay only a few feet away, but when she reached for it, the man simply kicked it away. Then Shell saw his other foot come up towards her face.

It was like nothing she'd ever felt. The man's boot connected with her cheek with enough force to knock her down onto her back. The warm iron taste of blood filled her mouth, and she spit the red stuff up onto the ground. She ran her tongue around, checking to make sure all her teeth were there.

"You son of a bitch!" Keon yelled.

"Easy there, Dark Meat," Cody said. "You'll get yours soon enough." He kneeled next to Shell and smiled. "You shouldn't have come back here, darlin'. Maybe now I'll let your friend here watch me fuck you before I kill him."

Shell narrowed her eyes as she looked up at the man. She spat a mixture of blood and mucus into his face.

Cody's smile disappeared and he stood up.

"You fucking bitch!"

He kicked Shell in the stomach hard enough to knock the breath out of her. She gasped as her eyes went wide, and he kicked her there again.

"Ray might have let you get away with that shit, but I won't."

Shell clutched her stomach and tried to crawl away. She grabbed a fistful of dirt, feeling the throbbing pain in her stomach with the other hand. Dirt flew into her eyes as the man's boot appeared next to her.

Cody yanked her upward by her hair, forcing her to stand despite all her pain. A hand wrapped around her throat from behind, and she felt the man's hot breath hit the back of her neck.

"You're gonna regret that you ever fucked with me," Cody said.

The doors to the barn opened then, and Shell fell to the ground as the man let her go. She fell face-first, the pain so intense in her stomach that she couldn't catch herself. Behind her, she heard a commotion, but she couldn't turn around to see what was going on.

Then there was a scream, and something hit the ground.

Shell pushed herself up enough to where she could turn around.

Cody lay on the ground, his face in the straw. He was motionless, and blood stained his blonde hair. Sticking out of his back was a sword. A hand grabbed the handle and withdrew the sword out of the Cody's back. Shell moved her eyes up to the dark figure's face.

The light was such that she could only see the outline of a trench coat and a cowboy hat. The figure moved out of the shadows.

"Dylan?"

It was him. He hurried over to Shell and kneeled next to her.

"You all right, kid?"

She spat more blood onto the ground, pushing herself up to her knees. "I'm fine. We need to get Keon some—"

"No!" a woman screamed outside.

"That was Katrina," Keon said.

He tried getting up, but groaned and fell back. Shell went over to him. Both of his knees were bloody and injured, keeping him from being able to get up.

Dylan went over to the barn doors and peeked outside. "Shit."

"What?" Shell asked.

Dylan looked back at her with his cold blue eyes.

"They've got Paul."

46

"Get the fuck out here!"

The man's burly voice came from outside and Shell knew instantly that it was Ray.

"I know you're in that barn. You better get your asses out here now."

Shell slowly stood, looking toward the barn doors. She started towards them, but Keon grabbed her leg.

"Wait."

"What?"

"Don't go out there."

She kneeled next to him and kissed him on the lips, cupping her hands around each side of his face. They were both bleeding, but it didn't matter. Shell wasn't walking out of that barn without kissing him.

"I have to."

Keon stared at her with blank eyes, tears welling. She turned away before she, too, grew emotional, and she went to the barn door. When she looked up at Dylan, he was staring at her.

"You ready?"

Shell notched an arrow back into her bow, then nodded at him. She raised her bow, ready to fire if necessary.

Dylan opened the door.

A group of people stood still, fifteen yards away from the barn. Katrina, Caleb, Julia, and Martin held their weapons aimed and focused on the same person Shell was focused in on.

Ray stood behind Paul with a knife pressed against his throat. He'd moved to where no one stood behind him. It appeared he was the last member of the gang alive.

"I suggest you put that down," Ray said to Shell.

"And I suggest you let him go."

Ray laughed. "You're joking, right?"

Shell kept the arrow aimed at the man's head. She breathed as Lewis had taught her.

"Do I look like I'm joking?"

"Put it down, Shell," Katrina said. "He's going to kill Paul if you don't."

Ray raised his shaggy black eyebrows. "Listen to your friend, sweetheart."

But Shell kept the arrow focused on him. Kept breathing.

"I'm ready to negotiate," Ray said. "You all done killed my whole gang. And we killed a lot of you in return. What do you say we work out a deal?"

"What kind of deal?" she demanded.

"That's easy. You let me go, and your boy Paul here gets to live."

"And how do I know that you aren't going to gather up more goons and return here to kill us?"

Ray grinned and shook his head. "I suppose you don't. But look around you. Enough of us are already dead. Do you really want more blood shed?"

"Don't do it," Paul said.

"Shut up, Paul," Katrina said, then looking over at Shell. "You've got to put it down, Shell."

"Yeah, Shell, come on," Caleb said.

"Don't listen to them!" Paul said.

"I should have killed you when I had the chance." Ray pushed the blade hard enough against Paul's throat to draw blood. "But I guess someone else's blood on your hands will be just as good."

"Stop!" Katrina said.

The man shrugged. "You got one last chance to convince your friend to put that bow down before my hand 'accidentally' slips and slides this steel across your friend's goddamn throat."

"Come on, Shell, you've got to listen to him," Julia said.

"Seriously," Katrina said. She was crying now. "Shell, please."

Shell looked into Paul's eyes. She could see that he didn't want her to put the bow down. He nodded, then closed his eyes.

Shell drew in a deep breath.

"Time's up," Ray said.

Exhaled.

"Say goodbye to your friend."

The others screamed.

Ray gripped the knife tighter.

Aim true and vanquish the past. End the pains of a life once lost.

Shell let go of the arrow.

It soared through the air, landing with a thud in Ray's right eye. He flew backward, and Paul cried out as the knife still slid across his throat.

Katrina and the others ran to Paul. He lay on the ground

with his hand over his throat, but when he let go, there was barely any blood coming out of the wound. The knife had only nicked him.

Shell walked over and looked down at Ray. He lay still with his arms spread, the arrow protruding from his eye.

The last member of the gang was dead.

Katrina looked up at Shell. She stood and grabbed onto Shell's shirt.

"What the hell was that shit? What were you thinking?"

"Katrina, let her go."

Shell and Katrina both followed the voice over to the barn, to where Keon had dragged himself outside.

Katrina hurried to her brother and hugged him.

Shell approached the rest of the group, who'd helped Paul to his feet. The knife had truly only grazed him. He was bleeding, but he'd be okay. Paul smiled, and tears filled Shell's eyes as she hugged him.

"Thank you," Paul said.

They pulled away from each other, and Shell noticed Paul's eyes looking over her shoulder. She turned around to see Dylan standing there.

Letting go of Paul, she went to Dylan and wrapped her arms around him. He embraced her, running his hand up and down her back.

"What made you come back?" Shell asked, pulling away.

"I guess I didn't want your last impression of me to be that I was selfish."

Shell smiled, wiping the tears from her eyes.

"We need to get you wrapped up so you'll stop bleeding," Julia said to Paul.

"Forget about me." Paul pointed at Keon. "He needs help."

"He's bleeding pretty bad," Katrina said. "We need bandages, or rags to stop the bleeding."

Shell turned and looked at her farmhouse. The light shined down on it like it had so many times before.

"I think I know just the place to get some."

EPILOGUE

One Week Later

SHELL LOOKED out the window of her bedroom as the morning sun watched over her front yard. Caleb was out in the grass being chased around by the kids. They tackled him and he fell to the ground as they mobbed him, all of them laughing.

She looked over at the barn, to where Julia was walking the goats outside. She set down a bucket full of milk, then led them over into the field to graze.

Everything was back to normal. It was like the days in the town before everyone had died. Shell was no longer alone. She had a new family.

She looked across the field at the farmhouse next door. In the window, looking back towards her, she saw a familiar face. Dylan stood in the window with his cowboy hat on top of his head. Shell smiled and waved, then turned when the sheets stirred behind her.

Keon opened his eyes, moaning as he stretched.

Shell grinned and looked back over to the house next door. But Dylan was no longer standing in the window. She shook her head, then walked over to the bed, sitting on the edge of it.

"Good morning." She leaned in and kissed him.

"Morning."

"How are your legs?"

"Didn't they seem fine last night?" he smiled.

Shell punched his arm. "Stop it. I know you were hurting."

"Nothing about that hurt."

"I'm serious," Shell said, shaking her head as she laughed.

She peeled back the sheets to check his wounds. The stitches had remained tight, keeping the wound closed, and the swelling had gone down some, even since the day before.

"I think these stitches might be ready to come out by the end of the week," she said.

"Sooner than that."

"Don't push it." Shell stood up. "I was gonna run downstairs. Do you want me to bring you anything back up?"

Keon pushed himself up and sat against the headboard. "Nah, I'm gonna come down there in a minute."

"You need me to hang here and help you down?"

"Nah, I think I got it."

"All right, just yell if you need me."

"I think I'll leave all the yelling and screaming for tonight."

Shell rolled her eyes. "Yeah, we'll see about that, Hot Shot."

She laughed as she turned to leave the room, but her eyes fell upon the wall.

One of the four walls in her bedroom was still covered with the marks representing each day she had been alone in the abandoned town. Ever since she had come back, she'd stared at it each morning, but hadn't added anymore marks.

"We can find some paint or something and cover that up," Keon said.

Shell looked back at him and smiled, shaking her head. "It's a good reminder."

Keon nodded in return and Shell left, shutting the door behind her to give Keon some privacy.

When she arrived downstairs, Shell headed left to the kitchen. Brooke was there, wearing an apron and portioning out the butchered meat of a deer that Martin had killed the previous evening. Shell crossed her arms and leaned against the doorframe.

"Really?"

"What?" Brooke asked. "You don't expect me just to lay in bed, do you?"

"You could let me handle this. Or Julia. Or Caleb. Or anyone."

Brooke waved her hand. "Nonsense. Besides, Paul has things taken care of."

Shell heard a coo and looked over to see Paul enter the room, holding his newborn daughter. Shell smiled and walked over.

"Well, good morning, little sweetie," she said, tickling the baby's belly.

The baby cackled, and all three adults in the room laughed. Brooke wiped her hands on the apron and reached out towards her husband. Paul handed Eloise over to her.

"I think she's hungry," Paul said.

"Well, we can take care of that. Can't we? Yes, we can." Brooke smiled and rocked the child. "Oh, yes we can." She drifted towards the living room. "I'm going to go sit in there where I can be a little more comfortable and feed her. Finish dividing this up if you don't mind."

"Yes, ma'am," Paul said, giving his wife a sarcastic salute.

Once Brooke had gone into the other room, Paul grabbed a carrot off of the counter and took a bite. He then looked at Shell and winked.

"Smooth move," Shell said.

"Eh, she'll live. We'll get more. Speaking of which, I was going to head out and work in the garden for a bit. Wanna come with? We can help Keon out there and make him watch us and feel helpless."

Shell laughed. "That sounds great. I just need to go say hi to someone first."

"Well, tell him 'hello' for me, and let him know that I'm gonna finally beat him in chess later on."

"I'll do that." Shell smiled and turned to the door.

"Hey, Shell."

She turned around.

"Thanks again. For everything. With Eloise being born and all, I've been so wrapped up in things that I feel like I haven't had the chance to be alone with you and say thanks."

"You don't owe me anything," Shell said. "You helped me get my home back. I'd say we're more than square."

Paul smiled, scratching his head and nodding.

Shell walked off through the back door.

She ducked under the clothesline full of drying garments and walked to the corner of the house. Two boys came zooming around the corner, nearly knocking her down. Shell threw her back up against the wall, avoiding them. One of them was the boy.

"Sorry about that, Miss Langford," Jimmy said.

"It's okay," Shell said, smiling.

She then turned her attention to the boy. He looked far different now that he was clean. All the dirt on his face had been wiped away, and they'd even found some better clothes for him to wear. With the dirt gone, his cheeks glowed red as he smiled.

"You having fun?" Shell asked.

The boy nodded. Then he hugged Shell, burying his head into her stomach and hugging her. Shell hugged him back with one hand and ran her other through his hair.

"Y'all better be running if you're back here," Caleb said from around the corner.

"The monster!" Jimmy said, grabbing the boy's hand. "We've gotta run!"

The two boys ran away, and Caleb came around the back of the house. He winked at Shell, then took chase after them.

Shell laughed as she watched him go after the boys. Then she turned away and started across the property to the next house over.

SHELL WALKED up the front porch steps of the two-story farmhouse. The home had once belonged to the Richardsons, but that had been years ago. They'd been an elderly couple when the world had changed, and had passed away seven years after. Mr. Richardson had died first, and Mrs. Richardson had lived only about six more weeks after becoming a widow.

The faded wood slats creaked as Shell went to the door and knocked on it. It hadn't been closed all the way, and it went ajar on the second knock. She pushed it open further and stepped into the house.

Looking around, she didn't see Dylan. He most often sat in the living room, lying back in the recliner with his feet up and looking out the window. Shell had spent several of the last evenings sitting with him. After having spent several days around people, Shell had found it difficult to return back home and live in the house by herself. The group spent most of the days hanging around Shell's, but retreated to their own homes they'd adopted around town in the evenings. So Shell had began going to Dylan's each night. They'd talked some, but mostly they'd sat in silence. That was the main reason Shell had spent time there. While she enjoyed Keon's company on the nights he stayed over, he talked a lot. That was okay, but there were times when she wanted to be in the company of another who just wanted to sit in silence.

And as she looked around the house now, she noticed the silence enveloping her.

She walked into the kitchen, and found it was empty. Checking the rest of the downstairs level, she found much of the same. Shell had just seen him from outside of her window. He had to be in the house somewhere.

She went up the stairs, checking the bathroom first before heading into Dylan's bedroom. When she passed through the open door, she stopped and stared at the bed.

Dylan's hat lay on the center of the bed. A note sat next to it with Shell's name scribbled on the front.

She didn't move. She just stood where she'd stopped and stared at her name. Sitting on the edge of the bed, she picked up the note. She unfolded it.

Shell,

*As you know, I'm not too good with words. Nonetheless, I
figured I might try to write something out to you.*
*I know you thanked me a lot after I helped you escape
from your house. But the truth is that you helped me. I
was nothing but a lost soul before we met. While I
thought I hid it good, you seemed to see right through me.
You were right. I was selfish, and that was all because I
was lonely and in a dark place. Much darker than you
know and that I let on.*
*But I see the light now, and that's all because of you. I
know it might seem strange that I am leaving after I just
wrote about how alone I was before we met, but I have
some things I just need to do. While there is light in me
now, there is also emptiness. I don't know if it will be filled
when I get to where I'm going, but I know that I have to
get there to find out.*
*Make sure the boy gets the hat. I think it'll be a good look
for him.*
*You're a good friend, Shell. Maybe we'll cross paths again
one day, but whether we do or not, I won't forget you.*

Dylan Farmer

Shell folded the letter up and clutched it to her chest.
When she turned and looked at the hat lying on the bed,
tears filled her eyes. She picked it up, then stood and left
the room.

When she walked out the front door, Keon was standing
at the bottom of the stairs. The smile on his face disappeared when he saw Shell crying.

"What's the matter?"

His eyes shifted to the hat and the note in her hands.

"He left, didn't he?"

Shell nodded as she walked down the stairs to meet him. Keon wrapped his arms around her.

"Did he say why?"

Shell pulled away and looked into Keon's eyes. She kissed him on the lips, then glanced over at her house.

The kids had moved back into the front yard now. Julia and Martin had joined Caleb in chasing them around. She looked at her house, where Paul and Brooke sat on the patio swing, him holding Eloise in his arms. She then looked back up at Keon.

"What do you say we go harvest some veggies for later? I'll race you."

"Haha," Keon said, shifting his weight as he held onto the banister.

She smiled as she took his hand into hers. She gestured toward the house, and they walked back there together.

Shell's heart now aimed true, and she had vanquished the past. Now it was time to live the life she'd once lost.

STAY INFORMED

Keep up to date with all my latest news and releases by joining my mailing list. Your information will never be shared or sold, and you'll never be spammed. I usually send out 1-2 emails a month informing you of new releases.

Click or visit:
http://bit.ly/zbblist

AFTERWORD

Thanks for reading Empty World.

This book has been a passion project I've been working on, on and off, for the past year or so, and I'm happy that it's now available for others to enjoy.

One of the biggest requests I get from readers is "Write more Empty Bodies!" When I was writing that series, by the time I got to the ending of Adaptation, the second book, I knew what the ending of the six book series was going to be. And I feel like Revelation brought a proper, satisfying conclusion to the series and the characters, so I didn't want to try to stretch the story of that particular group on any further.

But another idea began manifesting in my head. I kept wondering what this world would look like 15, or 20, or even 30 years after The Fall happened. What would people be like? How would they be surviving? What would the world look like? Will there still be Empties around?

And with that, Empty World became a thing, and I started to work on it.

I hope that you enjoyed revisiting this world with me. I

owe a lot to you, the fans of Empty Bodies, as you are a huge reason that I went from a guy working in a warehouse with an idea for a zombie book to someone who is now writing full-time and able to support my family with my books. I sincerely can't thank you enough.

So what does the future hold for Empty Bodies?

At this point, I'm not sure. I have some ideas of how I could continue writing in the world, but I haven't started working towards anything yet. I am in the midst of writing several series with J. Thorn as part of our Molten Universe Media partnership, so I've had to focus on those projects when not working on this.

There are several ways you can show me that you want more Empty Bodies. Leave a review on the site where you bought the book. Tell your friends about the series. Those are the two best ways, but you may also reach out to me personally if you would like at zbbwrites@gmail.com.

Furthermore, I would encourage you to join my mailing list to stay up to date with all the things I'm working on. That is where I reveal news first. You can join by visiting: http://bit.ly/zbblist

Thank you, again, for reading.

Zach Bohannon
August 17th, 2018

ALSO BY ZACH BOHANNON

For a complete list of books by Zach Bohannon, click or visit:

www.amazon.com/author/zbohannon

ABOUT ZACH BOHANNON

 Zach Bohannon is a horror, science fiction, and fantasy author. His critically acclaimed post-apocalyptic zombie series, Empty Bodies, is a former Amazon #1 bestseller. He lives in Tennessee with his wife, daughter, and German shepherd. He loves hockey, heavy metal, video games, reading, and he doesn't trust a beer he can see through. He's a retired drummer, and has had a beard since 2003—long before it was cool.

For More Information
www.zachbohannon.com
info@zachbohannon.com

Printed in Great Britain
by Amazon

80415825R00155